THE BOOK OF SAUDADE

AKSHAT KHARE

Made with ♥ on the Notion Press Platform
www.notionpress.com

Sitting here writing things on paper,

Instead of sticking the pencil into the air.

Bob Kaufman

Contents

CHAPTER ONE

ROOM 1202 AT THE GRAND HOTEL ABYSS

I check into The Grand Hotel Abyss. I slip into it on long forgetful walks, when the last drops of rain fall from the grey evening sky.

The Hotel is a place for the Castaways of the soul, for the Junkies of Dreaming, for all the Rejects of the Real.

Its hallways are always empty, and you never run into the other residents. Every room in the hotel is closed off to me, all of them but my own. This is the one and only rule of this place. We are, all of us, entitled to our own misery, and hold the keys to our own understanding of that misery.

My key reads 1202.

Nothing ever changes in The Grand Hotel Abyss. Maybe because there was 'nothing' there, so the idea of change never really applied to it. People slip in and they slip out. Most of the residents are never heard from again. Those who do return, have either forgotten the details of their stay, or have forced themselves to forget them.

The Hotel does not come cheap. The rooms become increasingly more expensive as one gets closer to the Abyss. The cost isn't always paid with money, although it helps if you have enough to afford a more comfortable flavour of Misery.

Sometimes, the residents choose to open their windows, stick their heads out, and gaze directly into the abyss. The chilling sight brews a storm in the being more exhilarating than all the thrills known to man, pleasures infinite in their subtlety. Some fall out, and in, from the nausea, others keep away from their windows.

The windows don't lock. They are always half open, always waiting for you.

I don't really know why I picked 1202. I have long forgotten how I ended up at the hotel, much less this room. I get glimpses of another room, at night, drowning in my solitude: Room 2402.

I asked the Bellhop the other day, if the room was empty.

"Not at all, sir, 2402 Is a very busy room. There is always someone going in, or coming out of it."

All roads lead to 1202.

The tea leaves and the coffee grounds in my spoon are the stuff of Life. I watch Time trickle by with every leaf, with every speck of golden brown dust.

The Hotel is a halfway house of desire.

A mind that has turned in upon itself is its own worst enemy. Things never get better, but they always manage to find ways to get worse. I am stuck in an unstable dream of a new stability. This dream is the limit of my world, a sanitized world, where all the risks are calculated down to the last decimals of chance and possibility.

I have momentarily escaped my misery in moments of perfect clarity. In stoic withdrawal, in Zen wisdom, in a whirlpool of the senses I have escaped countless times. But I always come back to it. I suffer from the Stockholm Syndrome of Despair.

There is a dishonesty to my escapes, it is the only reason I can think of why I always find a way back to my anguish.

The torture of my soul is a narcotic to my becoming.

I have given up on depths, those vicious Chimeras of the Soul. And this is neither a cause for rejoice nor for despair. Deep down, we are all the same; the same filth of narcissism, egoism, hedonism, and a boring sense of self-righteousness make us all. I will take a nice surface over that any day.

I believe there is a 'Façade of Depth' between these two, surface and true depth. This is the Goldilocks zone of our existence. A lie we tell to ourselves, and to others. The beautiful structures and palaces of 'us' wrought from the stuff of dreams, into a person, a person who walks, and talks, and occasionally even manages to smile.

What does the act of creation entail; do we sculpt ourselves out of the same primordial rock that was meted out to us? We spend our lives tirelessly chiselling away in the hopes of transforming it into something that is transcendentally 'us.' Or perhaps we are trying to pull ourselves out of some primordial swamp, slowly and painfully scraping off the muck that sticks to our skin, hoping to be finally rid of it, to be clean, to be ourselves.

Diving into this ocean of the unconscious to search for some deeper hidden truth is an endeavour whose mundanity is overshadowed only by its futility.

In my hopelessness in the face of the realisation that I can never leave them, I have fallen in love with Delhi, with Noida, with Home, with the carpets and the doorknobs of my exceptionally ordinary Grand Hotel Abyss.

Over time, I grew tired of the compromises that had to be made on the size and the ambition of my dreams. It ended with me giving up on all of them. I was free.

As these passed through me, and I flitted in and out of my soul hotel, I watched a swiftfoot bum walk by me. His great brown coat in tatters, his beard weighed down from his babbling rambling cacophony, his fingers dragging slow through the thick air, opening the fabric of the universe.

I meander around like the bum, thought clouds rumbling inside, and the city open at my feet. The roots of my soul have a strong hold, Atlas holding the sky on his shoulders strong hold on Delhi. They hide invisible, subterranean, holding me to my city.

All the imponderable Friscos and New Yorks of the world that float desolate, on islands in my imagination cannot replace the Delhi that roots me. After all the grunts and the grimaces, side looks and unasked-for glances have exhausted themselves, Delhi is still left standing. Even if it is only in its damp black cafes or chalk graffitied ruins.

I don't think it matters if I feel sad in the metros of this city instead of someplace else. I don't see the point in trading them in for Mumbai locals, or the Kolkata-Frisco streetcars of an era bygone.

Room 1202. Room 2402. Room 1102.

All of them are rooms at The Grand Hotel Abyss. Different times, Different places. But the people never change.

As much as I hate travel and movement, it becomes at times intolerable to wallow about and drown in the murky uncertain depths of my soul. It is at these moments when movement brings me out of my stone silent meditation and my feet carry me forward, thinking and rethinking the path on their own whim, as I slip into an active non-being. An observer of my own life, as it slowly unfolds around me.

Through the plate glass I watch as the terrain opens up and closes down, till at last I am faced by the boxcars of the universe, left to their dreamless slumbers, standing still in rail yards, dozing off in the cold night, wrapped up in the fabric of forgetting. I watch the now silent railyard trainwash that goes three kilometres per hour, and not more, slower than the snowfall in winter and more leisurely than cherry blossoms in spring.

The infinite yards end and give way to the sewer of all gutters, black from the wastefulness, which gives way to perfectly planted rows of cotton or India blue, a patch of dirt between the Sewer and the Yamuna. And the river black in its own sense, black from the ashen dead in her waters.

The green vines on the electric towers have now turned brown and the rot of life now lies heavy on the rust of death.

There is dirt at the bottom of the glass I'm drinking from. I try to clean it out, but it sticks to the glass.

If we manage to find a light at the bottom, it is nothing but the angler fish of delusion luring us In with its blinking light. We are lost little fish looking for something on the lightless ocean floor.

But what good is a surface?

I have settled for a compromise, the shady deal of the soul, a centrism of the spirit. The only way I can bear this Is through the routine everydayness of existence. The banality of everyday life is like a star holding us in its orbit. We can bear it, because we feel that the tangent of escape is always in our reach. But it never is. On and on we circle around our lives as the days blend into each other, lost to us. Dark rocks of fire and dirt, we the forsaken planets who are less than nothing without our dull stars.

We create and accept an idea of who we are and try to come to terms with our dark thoughts and disquiet fantasies. This idea helps us make our decadence acceptable to us, and perhaps even desirable to others. It is in this edifice that our being rests, the ever shifting complex of our becoming.

I have given myself over to these ideas. Show me an image that I desire and I will accept what you've chosen to leave out of the frame.

It is a little disheartening when I apply this notion to myself. I am the puppet of all strings; I am pulled apart by unimaginable forces. And my proud heart registers each pull of the string as a push from my own will, a push of my conscious out into the world. And just like that, I feel free in my unfreedom.

I went by on a stroll along the hotel corridor, and as I was making my way back to 1202, I spotted a half-open door with soft yellow light shining through and lighting up the dark hallway. I slowly tiptoed forward and leaned in to get a better look.

A man dressed up in a handsome blazer was sitting on a stool with his back to the door. He was grumbling to himself in front of a large canvas that, I realized to my horror, he had nailed to his window. It seemed to me that he had just washed away whatever was painted on it. Some traces of the paint remained. I quietly closed the door behind me and left him to his metaphysical finger painting.

I came back to my own room and looked at my dusty window. Equations, unfinished sentences, Ancient symbols of now dead languages, and other things half thought-out were carved in the dust.

I am tired of the plagiarisers of my life. There was a time, when I'd let people peek in on my dust carvings, my books, the inner workings of my soul.

That time is long past.

At night, sometimes I find myself on my feet, and I can't recall what call to action could have removed me from the comfort of my bed, I stand mute and stare dumbstruck at the spot my becoming possessed not so long ago.

I try to remember what it was this time and decide to give up. I shake my head and decide to fix myself some coffee. I slowly move to the kitchen and start shuffling things about. I quietly look at the tiny bubbles that come up on the surface of the pot and fizz out. They form small galaxies that spin around and change and froth, and finally vanish, without a trace.

I pour the milk in, and the coffee goes from dirty brown to a pleasing shade of caramel. Before I have a chance to indulge myself any more than usual the coffee curdles. I take one last look at the now spoilt brew before throwing it away.

My current schedule allows me to be out and about at odd hours of the day. And by odd I mean those perfectly normal hours of the day that we spend hunched over inane documents and unending spreadsheets. It is at these hours that I see old men lazing about in their three piece suits, brown shoes, and fedoras or Kurta-Nehru jackets of calmness. I can't help but feel pangs of envy when I look at them. Lives lived out to their inevitable end; Candles that lacked the audacity or the imagination to burn at both ends, short stocky candles drooping low with the wax of their years. Their wrinkled skin in folds, gathers at the bottom of their tired faces. The horror of the dross dull time that lies in wait for me has given me many a sleepless night.

All nights blend into each other as I watch the shadows dance across my ceiling. The solitary cars on the dark asphalt rumble by, their lights move slowly across from one end of the ceiling to other. When the guards take their rounds; the regular beat of their bamboo walking canes helps me mark the hour. And I pass my nights with the same tired sensibility which drives old men to stand on platforms and wait for trains, even when they don't have anywhere to go.

Interlude

What happens when an infinite summer wanders about in an unending winter?

The summer is a traveller, lost, under the stillness of stars not yet born.

The great summer of my life is almost at an end. This summer of uncountable winters, unforgettable pours of solitude and slow contemplative falls, but a summer all the same.

Sometimes when I am walking around the city, I wonder if anything really is there. I look at the ground, and I can see right through it. Other times, I see shark fins circling my feet on the tarmac.

I stand and look at the quadrilateral formed by the bridge, the road, and the walls of the garden against the horizon. And for a moment, I feel as if there really is something there. That there is a certain tangibility to the concrete, metal, sweat and blood. A belonging, even if it is to an illusion. I look at all the blank unremarkable faces around me, and I ask myself, how many of them are checked into the Hotel right now, at this very moment?

Stuck in their lives, escaping into some quintessentially forgotten sentiment, laundry drying out on the highway rails, a stop sign at the road, on a turn that no one takes. In my soul, it was almost spring, but not quite.

At times the temptation of 'finding myself' overtakes all conscious thought. In a flash, I am under the dark milkyway river night sky and on the edge of an epiphany. I feel the ecstatic glow of the amber streetlamp yellow on my face, followed by the sinking sadness of the unavoidable 'losing myself' that follows any revelation, divine or otherwise.

My melancholy soul sticks to me like carry-on luggage on the flights of my imagination.

I would regret all the wasted nights spent staring at the nothingness of this world in the cold on my balcony, if I knew how to regret them without forsaking the man I have become.

I look inside myself, and try to reclaim, patch by bloody patch, the lost terrain inside my mind. It is a cruel fate, of having lost oneself to the abstractions conjured in the mind. Ideas can be very dangerous once their seed is planted. They occur out of nowhere and take root in the antipodes of the sub-conscious. Then they start revealing themselves, in inner soliloquies, in stray daydreams, and eventually in our words.

Orpheus of Existence

Should I turn around and take a look at my own non-being?

I am walking the narrow stairs, trying to climb my way back to the real. And all I have to do, Is not look back at her; Eurydice of my Dreams, who dwells inside me.

I look up from my Journal, and let my gaze go about lazily over the people sitting in the rooftop café. The furniture is old and worn out, stained with use. The décor of the place is defined by psychedelic prints of Buddha and Shiva on cloth that hang over the damp walls.

A girl walks in and stops after three paces. She's dressed in a long knee length wool overcoat and boots. She pauses and turns her head to look at the sky and the mouldy buildings that define the horizon. Her eyes shift back to reality, some unfinished thought still heavy on her brow. She proceeds to walks over to the kitchen, poking her head in through the make shift curtain door. The manager steps out and greets her with a smile. They make their way to the table facing mine and sit down. She's sitting with her back to me. The top half of her hair are dyed bubble gum pink, and the bottom half dyed in the shiny green shade of raw mango toffee of now lost childhoods. The waiter brings them both a beer. And they start talking about something but I can't hear them.

My friend joins me and the evening drags out its leisurely course. The manager has left her now, and Ms Bubble gum misery is listening in on our conversation. I tailor my words to entertain her, as my friend throws confused looks my way.

The girl writes something in her little notebook, and I smile to myself.

There is a solitary blue lightbulb sun in the sky.

I marvel at the neon pouring through the crisscrossed bamboo partition, caught in my dreams of vodka women who sigh through their winesoaked teeth. These dreams echo out their banality in my life like wornout torndown cigarette metaphors. But the cigarettes never end, and the metaphors live on.

The man sitting two tables from ours has just ordered his second beer. He sounds somewhat European. There is a certain Baltic lostness in his face. He has a small notebook open at his table. The pages are fluttering in the wind like a mad butterfly. His beer arrives, and he flattens the butterfly with it.

I am surrounded by these strange hermits who have left their lands and come to mine. I see them in Delhi cafes in beer pint and ashtray misery, on sidewalks in Rishikesh with their knapsack kitchens and their sleeping bag beds strapped on their backs, scribbling away in their eternal little notebooks.

They stare deep into the cool choking sky, into the foaming rivers, rivers which remind them of their Seines and their Amazons, and back to the unchanging starry sky we all share equally. They turn their doleful deer eyes back to their notebooks, and write.

I look at them, and pen something down in my journal. And on and on it goes.

I have always known that I suffer from a delayed consciousness of life and the world around me. And I know that I lack the tablecloth that covers the mundanities of life. I may lack the emotional fabric, but I don't lack the substance of the fabric itself. My life catches up with me and I'm cast into the whirlwind, tornado onslaught of my violent thoughts. I am flung through the entire emotional spectrum in a few seconds. And as soon as it passes all is quiet again.

I scream hopelessly into my pillow, giving up on Hope. And yet I wake up, and go about my day, only to return to the pillow, again overcome by the useless desire to cry.

There is a woman who lives down in 1102.

I have never met her but I know that she is a poet. She is a poet but she never writes down a word. Instead she imbues her life with her poetry. She does not believe in condemning her poems to ink on parchment.

It is perhaps, a bit cruel, to have the artistic temperament, but not the talent. But far more inhuman, to possess talent and have nothing come of it. There are however secret consolations that make this state of affairs a little more bearable. Silent declarations that help us go to bed at night; "I would have been great, but I'm not understood." Or "I don't want recognition, It is only in anonymity and unfreedom that I'm truly free to create." and so on.

I think my coming into contact with her is an event in my life. Where we go from here is in the realm of the unknown. I don't think it'll end well, since we contacted each other out of an ineffable desperation, a Morse code born out of desire. The desperation of our solitudes crowded with loneliness.

Sometimes I climb over the walls and look down at the solved labyrinth under my feet. The city locked in its shadows and lights. I watch the people small and indiscernible bum about the maze and each other in a Brownian motion of people. Sheets of sounds that encased the panorama of their lives covered me as well, as I came down and lost myself in them; ambulances ringing their sirens ferrying the dying down service roads that lead nowhere; injured dogs quietly whimpering in pain under benches, visibly forgotten, the sickeningly sweet scent of death.

I try and shrug off visions of metros crashing into the rivers of people flowing about their day. The silence before the crash lies heavy in my mind.

We spend our lives walking around, looking for something that would give us happiness, if only for a moment. When we find these silver linings of clouds more morose and darker than all the storm clouds of the world, we start unravelling them.

Things that have happened to us, the monotony of the every day and we ourselves, are the architects of destruction of every joy available to us in life. I suppose that the stone pushed uphill, must roll down again.

Sometimes I think about that which gets stuck on its way down from my head to my heart. My heart unchecked by the poison of rationality goes on dreaming happily.

Once the clockwork simplicity of life is broken, it's impossible to restore it. The tiny ratchets, springs, wheels, pinions and gears that once worked in harmony, a hidden complexity behind the face, no longer keeps the time. A small bend in a gear tooth and it all comes to a stop. And we are left with nothing but the consolation of a broken clock being right every once in a while.

Sleep is the only solace one has in life, long dreamless sleep wrapped up in death's liquorice shroud. Dreams are better enjoyed when one is wide awake. Losing this oasis of existence leaves me inconsolable, watching the hours pass by with nothing to fill them with. I struggle to piece together my hazy recollections and blurred concepts into a lucid whole. All nights eventually blend into each other. Sometimes a pack of dogs passes by, barking and fornicating. Solitary cars on the dark asphalt rumble by, motorcycles kick start without a warning, the vibration of my window as the cross-country trucks roll away, finally vanishing at the edge of this nocturnal soundscape.

And sometimes not any sound but that of the leaves rustling in the wind and the room heavy with my breathing. Some nights leave you scrambling over the wreckage in search of the rising sun.

Mornings that follow sleepless nights, leave me with a greater awareness of the things around me. I decide to go out of the house for some tea. The daggering light stabs my eyes. There is a certain strangeness to the ordinary everydayness of the world around me. I can't immediately identify what tit is that is strange. The kids had left for school and their parents were buying milk and bread. I realised with a jolt that I hadn't been out at this hour in years.

The tea stall was already bustling with business. The local madman was also at the shop getting his free tea. I paid for the tea and crossed the street to my tree. The tree after years of supporting people's backs had worn down and was rather comfortable.

The bum at the stall was muttering a mantra into his cup. He then slowly proceeded to take a sip. The sunlight bathed the morning in its warm yellow glow slanting through the sky. A dog trotted across the street, sauntering past the traffic which parted around him like the red sea.

I looked back at the crazy bum, who was now preaching a sermon at me from across the street. His eyes fixed on me, with a hint of contempt on his face. He grumbled some more and took another sip. I went back to my cigarette, slowly sipping on my tea wondering if I should mumble a mantra into my cup as well. A truck carrying the rent tables of old worn wood and browned out metal passed by, clickety clacking about its day; last reminders of the weekly market stalls.

The bum crossed the street and stopped a short distance from me and then took a sharp turn, and sat on the bench. He took off his slippers and folded his legs. His long scooped toenails hung over his broken chappals. The Mad Yogi began his rambling urban meditation sutra anew.

Phenomenology of the Damned

Do the damned owe us their thoughts, their inner demons and the monotony of their damnation?

Some of us task ourselves with the grand crusade of reclaiming meaning and all its associated burdens from the murk of our collective unconscious. The consciousness that springs forth from our mild albeit subtle discomforts. Is there any value to these sentiments, to the vague notions that come to us when we dabble with despair?

We aren't the condemned or the damned, but are the Dreamers of Damnation. We dabble with addiction to understand those condemned to the needle; we starve ourselves to understand the desperation of starvation. We struggle with our abstractions in our attempts to understand the dreads and the passions of the truly damned.

There are people who are denied the luxury of articulating their misery, much less that of penning them down.

When we write down what we feel, the immediate effect is that of a psychic cleanse. The quickest way I have to rid myself of my thoughts, is to write them down. The long term is a shared solidarity with others; a brotherhood of people who had the same struggles and shared the same sensibility. I have paperback conversations with them, and they've helped me get through many an uneasy night.

To bear this burden silently, not as a choice but as a fate, feels like a noble undertaking when looked upon by the eye of abstraction. The reality of enduring meaningless suffering is drastically different. Men dying in the service of ideas that they don't really believe in, children who haven't learned the alphabet yet, out in the streets starving under the glaring sun, entire countries torn apart by disease and death and war.

There is a horror that passes through my soul when I think of all the mute suffering that was never articulated and still 'is' trapped in the decaying flesh in the ground or floating in the human ash dust that settles on our books, clothes, and other neglected corners of our homes and our minds.

I don't hope for much. But I do hope for understanding glances of a shared friendship, for sideway looks from a lover, when she is talking with someone else, letting me know that she is with me. The shared looks of amusement with strangers, when something unexpected happens on the bus. I believe these are the moments of pure communication that redeem us.

I hope for this as I meander through my life's tedium, through its stiflingly heavy afternoons and humid mosquito evenings.

The road racing away looks like a harp playing soundless music. The changing texture of the road flows in waves of notes plucked skilfully by the player. Gravel bounces against the underbelly of the bus producing a soft clinking sound every now and then. I focus my eyes back on the glass of the bus window and see the dark bags forming under my eyes and small red veins climbing their way to the irises. I rub my face to get the blood flowing again. Sometimes I forget that I have a face. The rhythmic whirr of wheels helps slow down the stupid freight train speed of my thoughts that comes from not sleeping.

I raise my head slightly and examine the girl standing in the front of the bus. She is dressed in a white kurta and has her headphones on, lost in her own thoughts. I am already in love with this image.

I collect images like objects. Sometimes I spend hours in the little darkroom of my mind. Developing these images in various baths filled with different ideas, taping them together, cutting them only to retape them. After hours of these operations I stand back and look at my work; a mesh of sensations and impressions illuminated by red light.

A telephone, a purple wall in a slum, a green typewriter, hands, spectacles, and people, all jumbled up in my mind.

In the clutches of these hazy recollections, I registered that the bus conductor was talking to someone who was in my seat. I started shuffling around my pockets for the fare.

Often I find myself marooned in my dreams; the dreams aren't abstract or formless. They take on some physical characteristics from the landscapes of my life.

The sad and insistent beauty of a painted landscape can only be appreciated as an image. When one is in the landscape itself, there is no comfort or time, unless it is in a dream, where time is more malleable and lends itself to us, to be used as we see fit. The non-linearity becomes glaringly apparent contrasted against the hazy nature of the dream.

My landscapes have names. Grand Hotel Abyss is the landscape of my disenchantment, my distance from the world as I move through it.

People walk around the city cast into their own concerns, their own silences. I watch them evoke different mornings and evenings as they barrel through the city in the shiny metros. Some of them must be in a place which is very similar to my Hotel, and yet fundamentally different.

Most of us are bogged down by the everyday tedium of our lives. Some are lost in the equally, if not more, tedious dreams of grandeur. Some of us look at the other passengers, the passers-by as nondescript puppets stringed through, most of us under the delusion of an unrivalled profundity, a delusion that borders on solipsism.

Nausea takes hold of my last conscious thoughts, and I feel my life slowly drip away.

With the closing of this season of my life, I often find myself going over the treasured secrets that spangle the fabric of these years. The uncountable shiny titbits that stand as a reminder of a life lived, and of a live remembered. I know that someday they will be lost to me as well.

Our secrets are secrets only in life. Trunks locked up with keepsakes, journals kept under lock and key, overflowing with confessions; the moment we die, they are flung out into the open and laid bare for all to see.

Even if we scream out our secrets in empty forests, after our death, someone will stumble on the echo.

I am in the market for a new soul. This one makes too much noise, and flies off in a hundred different directions all at once. It tries to dream of all things in heaven and on earth, and having failed, sits in a corner resigned to its fate.

Although this is madness, there is a method to it.

The loss of foundations, of inner terrains of the spirit has led to this. What the mind fails to find in itself, it searches for in the world of sensations and things. And it will haunt the world till the time it has reclaimed what was lost.

Although this is madness, there is method to it.

Sometimes I consider raising the white flag of defeat in triumph. There is purity in rebelling for lost causes, the romance of rebelling against an eternal defeat. The white flag to me represents an infinite potential for rebellion, it can be dyed any colour and raised again, bright flash of white fabric made from the stuff of our dreams. The world we live in never ceases to amaze me; even a tiny speck of dust in the cosmos can dream of burning brighter than all the stars in the night sky. And it is in dreaming that we are all equals.

Before summer ends and the rains arrive, the late afternoons are painted in dulcet colours of red, and the air lies heavy with nostalgia. These evenings call to my mind the images of women sitting together in cafes, all hair and hands, of men pacing outside bars waiting on their friends. I think of the rejected invitations and the clumsy excuses I have provided for not joining them. The monotony of these evenings frees me from the unending cycle of thoughts that devour all other thoughts, and having no sustenance left, eventually themselves. I breathe a little easier and lose myself in the nostalgia of times now past, and times that never were.

The wax stamp of my experiences lies heavy on my mind, as I regard the neighbourhood cricket match unfolding downstairs.

Soon I will be on the road. Neatly painted walls of imitation and sadness will fade out and the white of badly plastered clay will take over the landscape. I will travel again along the well-trod road with tall eucalyptus trees planted on both sides that shine sometimes white and sometimes red under the headlights of the bus.

Because of who we are, and because of who I am, I understand that I am returning to that which I am leaving behind. When the road ends, new walls of imitation will fade in.

Summer's End

The last hours of the summer of my life are ticking themselves out. Watching the clock move through the minutes is an impossibly oppressive undertaking. But that is altogether more agreeable than trying to fill them with things and events.

The things to come are tugging at my elbow, calling my attention to them. It's almost time for me to leave this city and go to a new one. A change of seasons is in order. But my heart is a mess of electric wires all meshed in and jumbled up in some old part of Delhi whose name I've long forgotten.

Delhi is an ancient oud being played by invisible fingers on invisible hands. If you press your ear to the ground you can hear them gently strum the music.

When I come back to this city, it will have changed yet again. The same way it changes every day. You cannot step into the same city twice.

The sun was rising through the motley group of buildings that dot the horizon. The soft silence was peppered with the occasional chirping of the morning birds. Mynas were flying in and out of my view, and eagles were gliding patiently in search of their breakfast. Clouds were gliding leisurely with the slow April wind, a drowsy slowness that was seeping into my bones.

The soul yearns to be everywhere on a morning like this one. I can be everywhere if I wish it. Never really being anywhere. I breathe in the sharp icy morning air at the Grand Hotel Abyss.

My soul bound to me, But not To Me.

I am slow boat. I am silent shore.

I am a forgotten tune. I am Jazz June.

I am a man of inaction.

No, that isn't right. It's too circular

I am Inaction. There, that is better.

CHAPTER TWO

Elevator Jazz in the Library under the Sea

The sea is a dirty red with brown thrown in. Elevator jazz rings out from under the surface. Books in the library under the sea get thrown off their shelves with every push and pull of the tidal dance between the moon and the sea. Quietly they pick themselves up and float back to their shelves.

My last oasis is drying up. I can't hear the notes underwater, and music slowly dies. Major chords ring out like minors, and the minors fizzle out without registering in my soul.

There is enough bad poetry in the world without me adding to it. There are enough dead sonnets and bad couplets to drown the world in ink. Everything I read, Is either bad or dishonest, and just like that, all poetry dies for me.

I don't think I will last long in Mumbai.

I walk the soft silk streets and the twisted back alleyways of this city; a celestial hobo searching for secrets that never were.

The reason I won't last long here, Is the Sea. The dark emptiness of the horizon as it waves up and down in its unending tango. I am filled with horror as I look at the murmuring sea, infinite and mystical, and I an echo sitting on its shore. I feel the urge, to turn my back and run. Leave the salt and the ocean sky behind, and never look back. I grit my teeth and push my face further against the ocean winds.

There is a secret emptiness in my heart. A hollowness in my soul. The absence of something vital. This is what draws my unthinking feet to the shore. I don't come here out of some misplaced hope of completion, or to restore some cosmic imbalance inside me. I sit here out of a sense of solidarity; I sit here to watch the ocean night collapse in on itself; two abysses staring at each other.

We stepped out of the café. She looked around for our umbrellas, as I looked for a cigarette. The dark torrential pour pattered down in the narrow alleys of Colaba. A bike jostled over the paving stones and turned around the corner disappearing into the liquorice night. Its red tail light glow hanging back in the alley for some time still.

Smooth jazz, modal, makes its way out into the alley against the rain beating on the windows and doors. Walking against the wind, we make our way out from the alleys and into the streets. I stop at a tobacconist and buy a lighter and a pack of smokes.

I light my first and watch it smoulder unsteadily, struggling in the weather. Despising myself, and respecting myself for the despise. When it rains, the streets reflect the amber streetlamps and the white stars, a crisscrossed mirror framing the city, aware of the sky and the storm.

I take in the colour and the lights, soaking them in through my skin, all the way through to my soul, feeling a divine regret for everything around me. Hypersensitive to the sound of rain on cars, on buildings and on the streets, the smell of the rain earth, sweet petrichor, leaves rustling on bowed down trees, and other sounds of the world swim through my sleep addled mind.

She's walking with me in the rain, lost in her own June dreams. We walk past a lone pizzeria, its neon shining red and yellow and white on the street, and past uncountable waffle stores with their shutters down, forbidding in the rainy night. Till at last I drop her off at the train station and hail a hazy cab back home.

On the streets, shadow people projected on the café walls and the ice cream parlours wrapped up in their cool smiles, float in and out of my vision. I wander with a drowsy sadness, melancholy at some unimagined sight or the other.

The city is open at my feet, a mouldy paperback with damp and sentimental yellow pages marked in pencil. I walk across it, letting my eyes follow its sentences, words, alphabets, without taking them in.

Shadows cast on the vehicles passing by. Shadows of women and men present there in the air, hanging for a moment before vanishing. As if they were hesitating to show themselves. My throat feels dry and my shadow a little heavier today.

Kitsch

This city's scrap dealers have a better haul than their Delhi counterparts. In the endless stacks of auction catalogues for artwork and sculptures, it's not uncommon to find the odd book on cinematography or art history.I pick up one of the catalogues and start thumbing through it; statues of copper, bronze, and rusted iron for the discerning collectors' drawing room. I start going through the other one, all of them indistinguishable from each other. The pain in my left eye started worsening in the dust and the mould.

I pay for my things and leave the shop.

The things that fall through the cracks in this city are different from those back home, and yet the same. Decadence here is a tall hatted foppish bum with a tilted cigarette, a frayed greyed overcoat and fingerless gloves. A city's second hand book stores are a good way to understand it and its people. I have in a matter of days managed to build a sizeable collection of Koestler and Bellow from the mounds of paperbacks, damp from the ocean wind.

Rainy Landscape

The land I walk on was once underwater. I breathe a little heavier under the weight of this realisation as I walk through the street of this modern Atlantis razed and reclaimed from the sea.

The seven islands now united under the unrelenting rain and the frothing ocean at the doorstep threatening to swallow up the city and its people. I imagine the hole in the wall newsagents and scrap bookers under the sea. Will the people even notice if it all happens quickly enough. Perhaps everyone will continue to bustle about their day. The locals would whoosh underwater, someone will come up with cigarettes that light even when underwater and everything would go swimmingly. Some, it goes without saying will look for a new prophet to part away the seas. I can't say when if ever this will come to pass, until then we have flat open mics and lifeless poetry readings to take up our days.

The fog of misunderstanding blurs out the colours and the edges of my world.

The night hangs softly over the stuffy ocean air. My impressions of the city are swirling behind my tired eyes. I am counting and recounting the square stones of the sidewalk as I meander across the blocks near the shore. I stop my foot mid-air and take a step back. I almost stepped on a man.

He is sleeping in the shadow of a car. The light from the streetlamp arches over the shadow and covers the rest of the sidewalk in its soft amber glow. His features are slightly visible in the darkness. The creases on his forehead that bear his life story are now relaxed. I look at his closed eyes and think about the dreams that flow behind them.

This man sleeping here, somewhere between church gate and marine drive, might be the greatest dreamer in the world. He is the only dreamer in his life, as I am in mine. And we are equals at least in dreaming. I hope for his sake that he is in a dreamless sleep. A long sleep without dreams does much to renew the spirit. He will dream again when he wakes up.

Realising that I have been standing over him for an unnaturally long time, I walk around him unknowingly quickening my pace. I slow down again, chiding myself at my naiveté. I was nothing but a dim shadow that disturbed him for a moment. He wouldn't have thought much of it.

I have lost count of the stones, so I begin again.

Most of this city's paintings hang in the display cases of abandoned storefronts, with only thin sheets of glass separating them and the street. Abstract Expressionist pieces, Madhubani patterns, Oriental fusions, all displayed together in a great mishmash of paint and canvas. The labels read thirty thousand, sixty thousand, fifty thousand, ninety thousand, a lakh-ten and so on. There is no risk of them being stolen. The mediocrity of the pieces and the ignorance of the poor conjointly insure their preservation.

All our lives are flavoured by the cold brewed bitter sweet ignorance that comes from knowing too much and yet not knowing enough.

The trains here are — different. In a metro there's often a decent chance of avoiding any contact throughout the day's travels. People spend their days bobbing and weaving through the crowds to avoid rubbing shoulders with anyone, with everyone.

This isn't possible in the locals. Almost every ride reminds me of the weekday work hour rush at Rajiv chowk; Times when you don't step out of the train but are birthed onto the platform by the horde of people rushing to their nine to five or the other way around.

The seats are also different; they are closer to each other, more intimate. I wonder how it affects the people here...

Every step in a new city renews the soul.

I lift my head to look at the stone archways and the trees soaked in the amber from the streetlights. My feet feel lighter as I look at the bright white displays of cafes and restrobars walking the endless road to somewhere.

The sun is stifling — oppressive. Old water pump shop owners and paper scrappers with nothing of note to sell are lazing about in the June heat.

The streets of Colaba are choking on automobiles. The traffic is bad enough that walking is faster if you were going to get somewhere. And I don't have anywhere to go or anywhere to be.

The rain saves me again. It falls down slow at first, steadily gaining pace, like a seasoned marathoner. It saves me from the violence I might do to others unchecked under the daggering sun, and it saves me from the violence I might do to myself.

Epecuén

There was once a city much like Mumbai, and perhaps nothing like it at all; a city that forged chains for the Sea.

There are whispers in its ruins, whispers of a boy who hid under hotel windows to listen to the music the tourists brought with them — whispers of the youth who cast the bricks for the city — bricks that lie stacked and unused — whispers of the man who thought he'd see it rebuilt when the water took over — whispers of the decrepit greybeard, Who knows it won't.

Epecuén — a city lost and a city regained. Two cities, separated only in time but not in place. Epecuén went under but something else surfaced, a spectre, the haunting dream of a city.

The dream of a city with benches and parks and hotels and cafes, and now a city with nothing. And yet a nothing that is more important than the somewheres and the somethings that were lost. It's a city revealed to us as a thing not present-at-hand but a thing-in-itself. It's no longer something that we can use, the city now, simply IS. It exists in itself.

The last man of Epecuén walks the streets turning over the unusable bricks to see if they bear his markings — to see if he made them. Pablo rides his bike with his dog through the streets of Epecuén as the wind rings out through the broken stone.

The libraries of Epecuén are no longer under the sea. There is no elevator jazz to numb the mind. The libraries are no longer under the sea. The books don't sway to the silent music of the ocean waves. The music doesn't haunt the water anymore. The libraries are no longer under the sea. And there is no music left to be made.

It's easy to get lost in the suburbs of Bandra. To my touristy eyes every block is indistinguishable from the next. I'm with a friend who's in the city for work. I don't think either of us has any idea of where we are or how to get back. The slow rhythm of my feet on the road and the unchanging scenery is making me a little drowsy.

We stop at a park that is built on the slant of a hill, with a nice little gazebo inside. A couple of kids are chasing a hen around the park. Two elder women are unpacking their lunches inside the gazebo.

I ask my friend if she wants to go in for a while. She nods absentmindedly, lost in some thought or the other.

I open my book and lie down on one of the benches under the trees. The bench slants with the park inducing a slight uneasiness in me. I breathe in slowly, trying to pay attention to the words.

Out of the corner of my eyes I can see her clicking photographs of the children, the trees, and the women.

The soft light of the blue sky filters through the branches and gently brushes my face as I flip the page of my book.

Years from now when I'll be walking the streets in the same suit that I'm wearing now, frayed from overuse and neglect of the wasted years — darned and mended in a hundred different places, the thread softly leaving with every turn of the wind; What will I think of today?

Today when the world is still open at my feet. Today when life is much easier and less dull and not as melancholy. Will I remember this day, or will it be lost in the monotone blend of everydays that we vaguely recall, but don't quite remember.

I catch my reflection in the neatly polished marble floor. A flash of despair passes through my mind at the sight of my unshaved face.

The last train is running a little later than usual. I feel my mouth go dry; the taste of loneliness bitter on my tongue.

The air pushes me back as the train stops at the platform. I animate myself and walk inside the carriage, drawing out the last dregs of hope in me.

Questions of how, where and why, have traced out their motions and now fade into the background; noiseless flies aching for blood.

Rainy Landscape

The salt water breaks over the tetrapods and sprays over the shoreline. Thunderclouds grumble lightning across the sky. The evershift horizon of black water waves solemnly glows under the thunderclouds in the sky.

Strangers to the right of me, Strangers to the left of me — watching the sea squabble with the night sky — sitting here, now, expecting private epiphanies, dreaming day dreams and impossible conversations. I taste the rum on my tongue and long for the Caribbean.

As I opened my satchel that night, I discovered that the sea water had found its way inside the denim. I emptied it on the table to examine the damage. All of the books had drunk in the ocean much like their owner. I smiled at the little irony, and laid them out to dry.

There was once a king with a kingdom that stretched out to the edge of all that was known. And although his kingdom stretched out to the ends of all that was conceivable he had no subjects. He had no subjects but one; Himself.

He was alone there, with nothing to look forward to but the passage of time in the vast emptiness of everything that was his birth right. In order to fill his time, he decided to make something of his kingdom. After hours of deliberation and reneging, he decided to lift it up from the ground and raise a fortress in its place. A fortress gilded with the best the land had to offer. A testament to all he valued carved in marble white.

Others might have despaired at undertaking something this ambitious alone, but our king was clever as he was crafty. So he set about to work and started stacking the stones one after the other, working tirelessly for years on end. It was hard work, and couldn't all be done at once. There were many mistakes made along the way. Sometimes he would build a column but then take it down and rebuild it because he spotted some minor blemish or because it didn't turn out the way he had thought it would. Other times he'd replace entire sections of the roofing because the tiles didn't quite fit in as he laid down the final one. And so in this manner, after building it and then rebuilding it, at last he stepped back to admire his work.

It was beautiful. The fortress stood tall at the heart of his world, its minarets stretching out to the sky, the marble standing resolutely over the surroundings, the aging silver softly shining in the sun. He decided to explore it.

As soon as he stepped in, the fortress started shaking violently. The king braced himself for an earthquake. But it wasn't an earthquake that was causing the vibrations. The king peered out of the window and saw a gargantuan hand trying to dislodge the structure.

Suddenly, the fortress was plucked from its place and flung out into the antipodes of the universe beyond the known. Tossed out in the void, condemned to float about with no bearing, for all time and no time, no up or down, north of no south, no western salve to remedy its situation, and no eastern solution that could return it back to where it once stood.

At first, the King could not understand what was happening. Where had he gone wrong? Where was his error? Disoriented and confused, he started navigating the halls one by one to chase out the source of this unbalance— turning over every brick and prying into every cranny. He searched and searched, day in and day out, but he could not find the cause.

The King eventually succumbed to madness inside the cramped walls, but there was no gravity for him to hang himself, and no air to carry his screams and now he wanders the halls, still searching.

This absence, it separates me from my life. On these occasions, I am a shade who has entered a novel. I can't sleep, I can't blink. All I can do is watch the tragedy unfold in front of my eyes, with no voice to protest and no tangibility to intervene.

My unwavering scepticism eats away at whatever little sand I manage to gather and mould with my hands. The ocean retreats, only to come back and wash over the sandcastles of meaning. Finally, frustrated at the poor material and at my own helplessness, I give up and bury myself in the sand to enjoy the sun at my face and the ocean at my feet.

The absence of work eventually itself became tedious, and so I go back to the sand. And like the ocean waves themselves, I oscillate between these two extremes, which aren't extremes after all.

I sit at my balcony in the dark of moon plains alone, or watch the sea awash with the bleeding moonlight.

My life imbibes the meaningless chaos of an out of tune brass section.

It imbibes the sadness of the men who play the weddings in India, marching in their over starched white jackets and pants in the sweltering heat of May nights. All year round I watch them carry dim chandeliers through the streets, blowing on their instruments. All year round, I watch countless men propped up on underfed horses, with a bag tied to their mouths for the feed, and another tied to their assholes for the shit. All year round I watch jumbled up feet dancing to the blare of horns, to the beat of drums with loose skin.

The only thing missing from their group is a little out of tune alto sax.

Sometimes when the moonlight pours over the dull throbs of oppressive humidity, I like to spend my time watching little birds flit in and out of view, appearing and vanishing out of dark patches of the night untouched by streetlamp amber and white lights. They remind me of this snow owl I once saw gliding across a park lost in the hazy uncertainty of my memories. The nights come alive with the rustle of the wind over the trees, the movement of the shadows over the grey concrete that was left uncovered. A different me opens the window and marvels at the tired old view, unable to sleep, but not sleepless.

But on dawns following nights of unbearable sleeplessness and indecision. The leaves move with the wind and the cuckoos' call washes over me, restoring so much of what the night had taken away. The soft light of the hours that follow light the dusty corners of my solitude, I get out of the bed and shake off last night's whispered anxieties from my quilt, fold it into a nice clean rectangle and put it away for later use.

The rest of the day is a hallucination. I walk through the beat down paths of my day, mindlessly repeating the same action, and no one catches me at it. From the hallucinations I slip into daydreams and from daydreams onto trains that shuffle around in my mind in circles.

The only time I can sleep without dreams is when I have exhausted the last spark of that anxious industriousness that tries to realise everything, and accomplishes nothing.

There's some peace to be found on the docks. It's a short walk from the causeway. The distance is filled with old houses painted in fluorescent shades of purples and greens that don't really go with the architecture. The soft sunshine tempered by the cool breeze washes over the whole neighbourhood. The streets are not very busy around the area, unless it's raining. Even a few raindrops hold in them enough potency to block all the streets of the city with shiny automobiles, and old premier padminis.

The shape of the land allows one to find the sea in all directions but one. And as you get closer to it, the tarmac starts changing with every step taken in the right direction. The black dull surface is encrusted with millions of broken seashells. The white shards safely tucked in between the tiny breaks in the road.

The storage sheds leading to the docks have been painted over with murals. The damp ocean air has more or less erased them from view. What little remains to be seen signals to the grandeur of what was lost, but there isn't much to look at.

The first thing I see as I enter the docks is a man sleeping on a heap of old coral blue netting by the lemonade vendor. He's tucked himself in, the creases around his forehead, less intense under the soft shadow of the shed. I buy a water bottle from the old vendor as he hawks and calls out to the men passing by, offering sagely wisdom and lemonade under the ocean sun. His hair is greyed out more since I last saw him, his skin grown more taut on his bones. There are fewer takers for his counsel now.

The ocean is closed for a few months. Rusty anchors are piled one on top of the other before the boardwalk. The fruit vendor has vanished from his permanent place but the old gas station is still here, its forgotten meters rusting from the ocean salt and water.

I sidestep to avoid the perfectly preserved shells that have made their way to the concrete floor next to the discarded playing cards; a ten of hearts here, a two of spades there. When the ocean is closed it becomes harder to kill time. Netters are working in neat little rows near the end of the yard, slowly taking the thin blue, green, coral lines and spinning them together for nets that can be used when the order comes in, and the doors to the ocean are finally open.

Around five or seven men are already sitting there with their legs over the edge as I walk in. Their fishing lines cast into the water and small plastic bags of bait lying next to them. I go to the edge and put my bag down on my usual spot letting my eyes soak everything in. The light house is a small blip on the other tip of the land, standing vigil over the sea in its now muted blind defunct solitude. The cats are swiping lazily at the crows who are hopping about nearby. They slowly glide back on the sea winds with their wings stretched out to avoid the cats, like small kites hooked to the ocean floor with invisible pieces of string.

I start talking to the man next to me. He is frustrated because he's not in the ocean. Because of the storm warnings, they're stuck here and have to make do with catching small fish in lowtide waters. He starts telling me about all sorts of things. How they sometimes sneak off at night to the Worli seaface to get at the bigger fish, and how it's not about the meat or the money. Just something to kill time and most of them are vegetarians anyway.

An old man walks to us and shows us a small broken basket, the kind used by vegetable vendors with crabs scuttling about in it. The crabs are the real enemies on the coast; they tuck on the line and eat the bait. The old man walks away, his complaints riding off in the air with the ocean winds. The man next to me pulls out his fishing line slowly and asks his friend for fresh bait. He dutifully pulls out a thin razor from the air. He handles the rusty blade expertly and relives the prawns of their shells. The cats swipe at the bait but are shooed away by him. All but the pregnant cat who slowly wanders off before lying down under the shadow of the small supply shed nearby.

I ask him if I can examine the fishing line. He warns me about the sharpness of the hooks as he hands one over to me. The line has few seashells on it, with two hooks below it, placed at some distance. In order to add weight to the line he has tied a door knob rose at its end. A coke bottle serves as the reel for this make shift fishing pole. The machimar hooks the bait on them, and casts the line again.

The hooks fly in perfect circles around the doorknob rose which glides through the air. For a moment I feel as if the rose and the hooks and the seashells are going to fly off and leave for undiscovered islands of the Arabian Sea, before they suddenly stop mid-air and drop in the water with a heavy plop.

A dark shape starts circling the hook, and the machimar reels it in with an expert tug. A burlap sack breathes fresh air after weeks underwater.

I caught my first fish on the third try. The tricky part of the whole affair isn't reeling them in, but casting the line properly. When I finally got it right, I felt the tug of life from beneath the water, and I jerked the line out excitedly. It was a small creature, and its tiny lungs gave up in a few seconds. Is taking a life, always this anti-climactic?

I throw my catch to the pregnant cat.

There's a tree stump in some forgotten corner of the world. It's covered in green moss and bracket fungus. In the untended corners of my mind, the stump unchecked grew into a forest; a forest of tall pines watered by the rivulets of my forgetting.

I wandered under the canopy of the starless night and stumbled back into the concrete forest that must have grown out of the chipped off cement from some back alley or the other.

Half-awake I look up at the masts of the broken ship in the middle of the street. The sails uselessly flutter in the wind, wrapped up in a futile struggle with the asphalt, hoping to find their way back to the sea.

The rocks around the boats hold fossilized sea shells. I pick one up, the dull white and brown shells lap over each other, their ends fused into the dull slate rock. I turn it over, and a single soda can tab is wedged into the smooth surface. I put it down. The wind is still sighing aimless through the sails.

I walk to the hull and run my hands over the barnacle and moss covered hull. The air is dry on my lips.

It was in the early hours of the morning next day, as I was waiting for the local that I thought about the ship again. I was looking at the dead end stoppers for the train at Churchgate. Slowly the rain that was trickling through the cracks in the roof filled the depressed vacuity that houses the tracks.

A decrepit old man was sitting at the edge of the platform. He had rolled up his trousers and had dipped his feet in the hammerhead shark infested waters of the pool. The sharks softly nibbled the dead skin off his feet. The sun was now shining in bits and pieces from the cracks through which the water had poured in.

He put a thumb to his dentures, whistled through all his embouchures before settling on one, raised his trumpet and blew the saddest tune that I will ever know.

He broke his own heart with every note, just so he could play the next one.

CHAPTER THREE

THE LAST GHAT ON THE RIVER OF FORGETFULNESS

When the world becomes too much for me, I sit and watch people walk into the moving water from the last ghat on the river of forgetfulness. I look at the green in the world and it helps my soul. Even when they're growing around warped wire, or rising out of the gutters; Trees with their leaves help me feel less lost.

Do we see the same green? Maybe your green is brighter than mine? Bleaker than mine?

There's really no way to find out.

The lanterns light themselves. I lift my head to look around the ghat. Floating above the river are a thousand corpses, covered in white cloth cut from the fabric of the dull moon that shines from behind the fog.

The river is almost silent. The night lies heavy on her waters.

What does it mean to me? It has been two years since my father died. What do these words strung together in a sentence, mean to me?

It has slowly been reduced to one of the many anecdotes of my life. I read this book. I have been to this or that place. My father is dead. The man no longer breathes in my words, I'm not sure if he ever really did. And it is becoming harder every day to remember him as he was in life. When I try to conjure an image of him, when I force myself to it, the only thing I can see, is him on his bed, his hands folded in, tongue caught in teeth, and my mother screaming out his name.

Losing memories is a second death; a second loss, something that rings louder and stings sharper in its finality. I don't have the nightmares of his presence anymore. Has he been lost somewhere in the antipodes of my consciousness?

Lost to my river of forgetfulness?

The drowsy calm of the morning is pierced by loud violent screams. Screams that fall on deaf ears; His and Mine, I close my book and walk over to his room. It is a short walk. Afterwards I've often wondered why it didn't feel like an eternity like it was supposed to. I walk over to him, and touch his forehead.

Cold.

Dead.

I know it's too late for ambulances and electric shocks to the heart. I go to the other room, and hold my sister to me.

My mother decided to postpone her breakdown indefinitely, because 'there simply wasn't any time for it.' She told us that she didn't have the luxury of losing her mind. She locked some of it away in a trunk and threw out the key. The remainder she parcelled out, in little mouthfuls to be taken every day till the end of her days.

I catch her sometimes, while she's quietly chewing the cud of her loneliness and washing it down with her tears away from prying eyes.

Rainy Landscape

The music of the rain on the metro roof tin sends a wave of nostalgia shooting through me — the soothing aroma of the earth mixed in with the rain as it wafts on the back of the gentle wind — the whoosh of the train as it cuts the stuffy air and takes its place on the platform.

A family is roasting corn under a tarp. One end of the tarp is tied to the father's rickshaw, holding it up. The little girl is trying to pick up the half cooked cob but keeps dropping it on the wire fence coal grill. Her mother breathes life into the coalfire with her resigned sighs.

The rain is slow and soft now. But stubborn, persisting in its pitter pats and patter pits.

Gradually, I notice the flat circle of my life traced out in the puddles on the ground. Dull moments indistinguishable from each other, were it not for their separation in time, space and sensibility — eventually I gave in to the fatalism of the ups and downs of unchanging flat time.

But things do change, or at least they seem to. The beggars from my childhood have changed their spots. The old man who was driven out of his mind by his solitude, now sits in a small corner formed by the platform. His incoherence is unchanged. His eyes are unchanged. His decrepitude has grown older under the weight of universal neglect.

And the idea of his life as a circle eternally turning on itself, always repeating with him out on the street seeking peace against the freshly painted grey pillars doesn't sit right with me. Maybe it's a point with zero dimensions. Zero dimensions that begin with meaningless humiliation and end in suffering.

The Ganges sings its millennial songs in the silent dead of night. She roars over the pandemonium in the day, raising her voice to match the commotion on the babbling streets. It is at night that she becomes contemplative and silent but never quiet. And it was at night when I found myself on her banks, entirely by accident.

The repetition of the forests that lead up to Rishikesh is broken by small streams of water that run in tiny rivulets across the land. It'd be easy to mistake them for drains if it weren't for the moss and the fish and the rippling water as it sloshes about in the tiny concrete channels. The water is clear and cool, they aren't big enough to carry the chemical runoffs of the faraway Hindon.

When the sign of the forest that repeats itself in wood and silence does end, it opens to a sleeping city. The city is sleeping, but not her people. The tea vendors are still out and brewing fresh pots for the rickshaw drivers and the rare insomniac gallivanting about on the streets. It took us a while to find a room, but as soon as we did, we dropped off our heavy bags and our lazy friends and were on our way to the Ghat.

Even in the middle of the night, the ghat isn't empty. Old babas are sleeping on their mattresses on the top steps. The same mattresses will host people for their meditation sessions come morning; tourists in search of nirvana. In one corner of the ghat are a group of men smoking hookahs on their way to mindfulness, and on the other corner a group of students who decided not to take a room in the city, and are now tucked inside their jackets on the ground.

A couple is standing on the jetty. The guy is trying to get her to do something that she's clearly not into. The jetty is nothing but a few steps of metal jutting out into the river, propped up by empty pvc barrels and metal fastenings. We start walking along the edge of the ghat, stopping only to skip stones across the river. They all sink in after the first jump.

We walk about for some time, trying to eavesdrop on the couple and the shisha smokers. Moving up from skipping small stones to big ones, then to pieces of sticks once we'd cleaned off all the stones, and once the small twigs were gone, onto logs that had gotten stuck in the jetty or under it. Getting to the logs wasn't easy and we almost fell to what would be our ice cold graves, but there was a warm satisfaction to watching them fly across in arcs and then land in the river with a big plop. And after all our jambling and the ruckus that we'd caused on the ghat, disturbing the couple, the smokers and the babas, we decided to sit on the riverbank rocks and meditate like good old mischievous bodhisattvas.

The city lights were flickering across the river like lamps struggling against heavy winds.

I am blessed with the horrible assurance that I will never meet the dead or the dying. I do so admire the former and sometimes the latter as well. Despite my admiration I'm relieved that through reasons of ontology and of geography, it shall always be too late. And I, whose shadow falls on the staircase, will never see them again.

Two Travellers on the riverbed (A Play in Two Acts)
Act 1
Two worn out skulls are sleeping on the riverbed.

They don't have any distinguishing features, and would appear to be identical except perhaps to the most distinguished phrenologist.

They are slowly regaining consciousness because of the debris falling on their heads through the water.

ROSENCRANTZ (hereafter "Ros") is attempting to communicate with GUILDENSTERN (hereafter "GUIL") by sending vibrations through the medium of the river water.

ROS: Is anyone home?

GUIL [Confused]: Hunh, What?

ROS: I was asking if anyone was home, a question that has now been rendered moot.

GUIL [Irritably]: What are you on about then?

ROS: I'm not on about anything, I suppose. I'm on the riverbed I suppose.

GUIL [With effort]: What river?

ROS: I don't know. Would you like to venture a guess?

GUIL [He reflects]: Maybe the Rhine or the Danube?

ROS: Are you sure we're on a riverbed? We could be on the bottom of the Øresund.

GUIL: The width and the flow would suggest a river. What's the last thing you remember?

ROS: Something about a letter and the king of England.

GUIL: Then it's settled. We're at the bottom of the Thames.

ROS: If you say so. [Musingly] Are we just reduced to skulls then?

GUIL: What?

ROS [Gloomily]: I mean, you and I, Is this all that's left?

GUIL: But, what else?

ROS: I think it's reasonable to consider the possibility that my femur could be engaged in a riveting conversation about metaphysics with your Humerus.

GUIL: That is a symptom of your mundane panpsychism. [Pauses] I honestly thought you'd drop it after death at least.

ROS: But are we? [Hesitant] Dead, I mean.

GUIL: Yes, Yes It certainly looks that way.

ROS: Yes?

GUIL [Feebly]: I mean, No. I don't know.

ROS: Well, I don't know either. [Reflectively] I guess we'll have to make do with that.

GUIL: With what?

ROS: With not knowing, with the understanding that there's something rotten in the state of our epistemology.

GUIL [sighing deeply]: Oh.

ROS: Do you remember anything else?

GUIL: I think we were flipping coins.

ROS: We could do that to pass the time? I can sense a lot of them lying about the riverbed.

GUIL: So how do you propose we go about flipping them?

ROS: With our hands of course.

GUIL [without gesture]: We don't have hands.

ROS [Despairingly]: Oh. [Silence]

At this point bigger stones start hitting their craniums through the water.

ROS [Angrily]: I wish they would stop. It's giving me a terrible headache.

GUIL: I don't have any hope in the English.

ROS: Say Rosencrantz?

GUIL: Yes Guildenstern?

ROS: You remember our daft friend who was always talking to himself?

GUIL: I recall it very vaguely.

ROS: It's just that, He used to nonce around talking to skulls an awful lot. Do you reckon they were conscious of it as we are?

GUIL: In the interest of maintaining constancy, they must be.

ROS [vexed]: Oh! Sounds completely horrible, I don't think I'd be quite able to tolerate that.

GUIL [looking around]: Say, When do you think this will be over?

ROS: I'm not really sure. I remember thinking many times before this that it was·already over; after every exit perhaps and certainly after our business with the king. I suppose it was in fact 'over' for the longest time, but now it has started again.

At this moment, oil lamps pass over them, floating on the river.

ROS [Admiringly]: Say Guildenstern, Can you see the lights floating across the river?

GUIL [Wondrous]: Yes, It looks absolutely stunning. It's strange; I just remembered dancing with a lady in the Venetian Carnival. She was a buxom little thing, Dressed in red, with the sweetest scent of daisies about her.

ROS: Was she wearing a black mask with red lines through it?

GUIL: Yes, Do you remember her?

ROS: Actually, That was me dancing with you. No one was asking you, so I exchanged my clothes with a street player for a few minutes.

GUIL: What?

ROS [Gently]: I wanted to cheer you up. You were rather morbid slouching in a corner by yourself.

They are cut short as a log crashes into them, removing Guildenstern's mandible in its entirety and knocking out most of the teeth in Rosencrantz's mouth. They are caught in the flow of the river and begin their journey downstream.

Act 2

They slowly come back to their senses, only to find themselves caught in a current that will take them downstream and eventually to the ocean.

GUIL [Indignant]: Just when I thought no further humiliation was possible, I've had my jaw knocked off my head.

ROS [With effort]: And my teeth.

Enter Fibula.

FIB [Highly excited]: Oh, hello there gentlemen.

ROS [Coldly]: Yes hello. And who might you be?

FIB: I don't really remember. So I go by Fibula.

GUIL: Is that French?

FIB: No, it's Latin.

GUIL: Oh, Very well. And where are you from?

FIB [Feebly]: Somewhere in India, I can't really remember.

ROS: My good man what are you doing so far from the Orient?

Fib: I don't know about the Orient, but we are still in India.

GUIL: Is this not the Thames then?

FIB: Of course not. We're in the Ganges.

ROS: Say Rosencrantz, I don't remember us making any voyages to India.

GUIL: No, Rosencrantz. I don't.

ROS: Why are you talking to yourself?

GUIL [annoyed]: What? Have you lost your mind?

ROS: What?

GUIL [With great restraint]: Never mind.

ROS [He meditates]: It's rather inconvenient, to be reduced to this.

GUIL: Death is an inconvenience. It is a downright tactlessness and a menace for the general public. The only consolation you and I have is that ours is only an inconvenience to us.

ROS [Sadly]: I don't know about you, but I'm sure there's someone who'd miss me.

GUIL: We don't know how long we've been gone Rosencrantz. Even if there was someone to remember you, they're probably long gone now.

ROS: You get a kick out of imposing your dreary outlook on everyone.

GUIL: I'd rather be burnt as a cynic than live as a pathological optimist.

ROS: There's nothing wrong with looking at the brighter side of things. Cynicism never achieves anything.

GUIL: Yes, but what has idealism achieved. We're living proof that neither of them works.

ROS: What then, a compromise?

GUIL: Don't be silly. Mixing custard and mutton is going to ruin both and improve neither.

FIB: I don't know that sounds rather delicious.

GUIL [Annoyed]: Surely, there must be a dialectical solution to this problem.

ROS: Or a contradictory one?

GUIL: A paradox is not a solution; it's an obfuscation of the real problem.

ROS: What problem?

GUIL: The hard problem...

ROS [interrupting]: Isn't that redundant?

GUIL: ... of consciousness.

ROS: Well, there's a good case for dualism, and we its prime specimen.

GUIL: On the contrary I think if anything we represent physicalism.

ROS: I wouldn't be so sure about that.

GUIL: Do you really want to get into this right now?

ROS: You're right let's agree on property dualism and call it quits.

GUIL: That suits me.

FIB: Might I add something?

ROS and GUIL [together]: NO!

ROS [Anxious]: Do you think the seeress foretold our fates?

GUIL: Grimnir's seeress?

ROS: The very same.

GUIL: Come now dear chap, I doubt we're of enough consequence to warrant a verse in her prophecy.

ROS: I believe we are of infinite importance. At least to ourselves.

GUIL: Yes but that isn't an objective statement.

ROS: Yes but that isn't an objective statement.

GUIL [Angrily]: Stop it!

ROS: Stop what?

GUIL [Coldly]: Parroting my words.

ROS [Hurt, Coldly]: The same way you parrot ideas?

GUIL [Violently]: I would smack you if I could.

ROS: Well lucky me then.

GUIL: I don't understand how you can keep on spouting that drivel given the state we're in.

ROS: The stars above are reason enough Guildenstern, to weather out the transmutations of life, however undesirable they might be.

GUIL: How insuff.....

At this moment Guildenstern was fished out from the river by an Aghori, who scraped off the last bit of brain tissue left in him, wiping the last traces of his consciousness out. Rosencrantz continued to go on for a few more days, but it seems to me, we might as well stop here.

Whenever the bridges that cut across rivers are carried away by the flooding waters, they rise again, stronger and better, more out of necessity than anything else. Ropes turn to metal as time passes and calamity strikes. It's easy to lose hours watching the river pass by under your feet. I have lost hours. I don't know of any better way to pass sleepless nights. The bridge mildly sways against the strong mountain wind that is making its way down south.

What was intimately known to me under the moonlight, is a stranger in the day. Now instead of the gentle sway of the wind it thrums and hums with the passing of feet and scooters over it. The crush of people carries me away from my usual haunt and floats me all the way out to the city markets.

The scent of camphor washes over me. It's easy to lose one's way in the endless rows of wooden stalls covered in garlands and red cloth, selling incense, cotton, rice, yellow pastes of turmeric, and vermillion powders with added cinnabar and lime. It took me a while to realise that I had gotten separated from the people I was with. Overwhelmed with the amount of effort it'd take to find them, I decided to let them find me instead, promptly ordering tea at the nearest vendor. I took out my novel and started waiting for the chai on his spare ottoman.

We have been given two gifts, but not in equal measure; the gift of not-knowing and the gift of forgetting. The gift of ignorance lets us spend our days under the warm sun with a bounce in our steps and a smile on our face. We lose our first gift almost immediately, some sooner than others. To lose it too soon is lamentable, but to keep it longer than it was meant to be kept is a far greater tragedy. And now the world is a darker, sadder place. Our second gift doesn't come to us as easily and to some it never comes at all. The things that we want to keep with us are soon forgotten, and the ones we want to be rid of, never leave us. Trying to forget something is an act of committing it to our memory forever.

Rivers of Forgetfulness

The act of forgetting is the laughter of life. And it's no wonder that every mythical tradition has exhaustive ways of bringing about forgetfulness. There are rivers that bring about forgetfulness. There are some that wash sins away, and others that grant invulnerability. When I watch the waters, it's hard to remember if I'm on the bank of the Lethe or the Vaitarni. Did I of dip my feet in the Ganges or am I sitting by stygian waters. All of them are the same, all of them another.

Sometimes I can't tell if it's evening, or if the clouds have hidden away the morning sun. My life comes up to me as an uninvited daydream. And in all this, there is some hidden meaning behind the clouds that eludes me, gliding off further and further into the sunset as I run behind them.

The people I pass on the streets here are mumbling to themselves. I can read on their lips their hopes and dreams and sometimes their want for bread and a bowl of soup. There are happy faces in the crowd; most of them are tourists in this town. As is the way with things, man is only happy as a tourist never as a resident. The happiness of a settled home is often lost in the everyday things that go into making it a home. And the dreams that were penned at the end of a long grocery list often get washed away with the rain.

The beaches on riverbanks are always cleaner than the ones on the sea. More so if the river hasn't made its way to the valley yet. The sea's memory comes and goes. It brings back what is better left forgotten. But a river never comes back to the glades it has left behind. It takes its waters pregnant with regrets and memories and pours them into the ocean. We have polluted the ocean with our bad memories. And I'm sure it takes great delight in dumping them back on us.

The garbage is the true face of our memory. It comes back as a reminder, and then it goes, and then it comes back again. We carefully select and curate our memories, our lives, throwing off what doesn't fit in with the rest, throwing off what is now ugly, what is now useless. And for some time it works. The backwaters of our minds are as expansive as our oceans if not more so. But the tides change for that is their nature. And once more, our clean cities are covered in that endless waste of memory.

The strongest fit of laughter that I remember experiencing came to me at my Father's cremation. In the shamshan that morning, two other pyres were scheduled to be set on fire around the same time as his. I think I was sitting on a bench across the pyres when an old man's sock caught on fire on the pyre ten feet from Dad's. He jumped across the length of the shamshan, skipping on one leg trying to put it out. Just when he was about to give up and had resigned himself to joining the dead that day, he found a bucket of holy water and plunged his foot in. After a few seconds of writhing the fire finally went out. To this day, I don't understand why I was the only one laughing.

Pantomime

The people of this city, of every city go through the cycle of their lives without paying any special attention to what they're doing or why they're doing it. If someone was to slowly chip away at the foundations of the city, first, taking off the roofs, then the walls and the stairs. They would still go about their day as they always have. They would climb the air instead of the staircases and shower behind non-existent walls.

Sometimes I think about the little girl who wanted to grow up to write obituaries. I wonder what drove her to want such a thing. If I could chart out her thoughts in time, where would I find the exact moment when that thought crystallised in her.

I have written some obituaries. Most of them for people who don't exist, some for those who did. It's a very dull thing when you come down to it. It's the repetition of the same thing over and over again. Some simple facts, a list of achievements and heirs, some well-turned phrases, perhaps even a catchphrase. Et voila you have your very own obituary. It's often considered rude to add anything more. Obituaries are after all for the living and not for the dead.

How strange it is to live through times when elegies are written for cities, for forests, for the oceans and for the glaciers.

You can look at their faces, you can walk their neighbourhoods, you can visit them in exile, but you will never know what a displaced person thinks and how they feel. It is simple enough to ascribe some feeling of longing or of melancholy regret to them, to their thoughts. Yes, simple enough. How far it is from the truth or how close, we may never know.

Somewhere in Rishikesh at the end of the world, there are a dozen or so empty ashrams. There were rishis who meditated there. A little later some musicians from the west who stayed there rediscovered the secret beginnings of music and time. And now with no tenants there, the forest is slowly taking root over the stone once again.

There are legends of a town where the dead are entombed in the walls. Its residents believe that the presence of the dead in their mortar and stone makes their homes stronger against the attack of the elements and those of the spirits.

In every house, there are two lives, two aspects of a world that never meet; the people living inside the house and the people living inside the walls. The dead like shadows often mimic the movement of the people outside, never quite getting it right. There is a distorted sense of malice in their movements; a distortion which to the discerning observer might reveal itself as candid reflection. Uncountable shadow strings connect everyone in the city, the living and the dead. And after all these years it is hard to remember who is pulling on the strings and who is being pulled by them.

The memory of all the things I have been, and greater still all the things I have pretended to be weigh heavily on my being. What can I do to get rid of this intolerable feeling? Make sentences. The endless task of sentence making helps me cast out looped thoughts and feelings on paper. Sentences that I string together into paragraphs; there isn't much difference between me and the rudraksh vendor on the streets of Rishikesh, who must be beading yet another mala under the sun even as I write these words.

The great tragedy of our lives is that we live in the present. I know there are people out there who think they're stuck in the past as are there are people who live in constant fear of the future. But isn't being stuck in the past just a way of being stuck in the present with a longing for the past? We feel trapped between two infinites, when the real prison is the infinity of a single moment, frozen eternally. Isn't our fear of the future experienced as a fear in the present, a fear of all the things that might go wrong in the totality of possible futures?

Our entire lives are spent in the present, denying it. It would stand to reason that the great horror of our lives isn't in being stuck in the past or the future, but in the present. And greater still is the horror of the understanding that we are in the present, eternally.

I tried swimming across the glacial waters of the Ganges. After riding the current downstream for a few minutes, I decided to attempt crossing to the other side. The shore didn't look that far off, so I dove in. My muscles quickly went into action, recalling the years I had spent doing laps in the local pool. It was clear to me quarter of the way in, that I would die if I didn't turn back immediately. The cold started creeping in though my skin and my lungs were on fire. The current subsided as I got closer to the shore. I switched to treading water, going in several times, before finally making it to the shore.

I asked a couple of the local kids who were sitting on the rocks by the shore if anyone had managed to make it to the other side. One of them lazily raised his head and said, "They go to the other side, but they don't come back."

The possibilities of a small town are more quickly exhausted than those of a big one. Every landscape no matter how unique ends up as the repetition of the same signs over and over again. Same cafes, same bars, same people drowning in the rivers, same people drowning on the streets, same streets drowning in the fog; everything is imitation. You walk about the roads and the river shores until one day you suddenly catch yourself wishing that the landscape around you was reduced to a postcard existence. Reduced to something that can be viewed as a memory of itself; a haunting that fits in the tiny spaces of your desk drawers.

We restricted everything we did to hotel rooms. They can't reveal anything about you to the other person. That isn't to say they are entirely without character. Most of them are shady and smell strongly of room fresheners. I think I can remember the rooms I've made love in more clearly than the people I've made love with. Sometimes empty spaces can wreck more violence on the soul than occupied ones.

I'm not sure that we ever made love to each other in all our times together. I might have made love to her in the beginning, and I think there were moments when she felt something weigh on her heart, but it never became anything more than that. It suited us, and neither of us hoped for anything more because of where we were in our lives at that point. Sex with her had the improvisational feel of jazz the first couple of times you did it. But over time I became painfully aware that there was nothing spontaneous about it or her. Everything was done in keeping with the standards stored in the songbook of her mind. It wasn't Chet on his trumpet. Only the repetition of the same notes coming from a scratchy gramophone. The needle dropped and we followed the groove of whatever record struck her fancy that night. Bad music is sometimes more restful than a worn out record.

There are some points before the big drops where the river gently flows through small cascades. Someone had the ingenuity to set up a table on one of the steps. We sat on the table, as the cool water gently flowed by our feet. The table cloth was soaked in the river water so we had to be careful with our cigarettes and the matches.

The real violence of existence isn't in death, it isn't in wars or famines or plagues. The real violence is ennui; the intolerable reality of our lives. Tedium experienced as tedium. Sometimes I lose weeks unable to leave my bed and venture out into the world. Other times I'm always on the move, working, writing, sleeping on my chair and never even reaching the bed. It is life lived as a constant dying. *Ennui.* Sweet ennui. It takes too much out of a person. The mundanity of being out in the world is no different from the mundanity of being in bed for weeks. Even the most beautiful sky is dulled by the grey tentacles of that feeling which takes over every part of your life. Its claws slowly cover in smoke the purest page of poetry. Everything is a futile attempt to fill time that refuses to be filled and stands obstinately as itself, or in the slow movement of the minute hand.

It was around this time that my drinking spilled over squarely into the area labelled a problem. I took to carrying around a flask with me everywhere I went. Or at least to places without metal detectors. Which is most places. I started losing time in a very different sense. It wasn't metaphorical or metaphysical anymore, it was literal now. I can't remember how many times I woke up in a bed thinking it was my own, with a blanket that I thought felt like mine, and felt a sense of relief at thinking that it was my own. But it wasn't. It was always someone else's room. And I wore borrowed pyjamas home. And spent the day tracking down everything I had on me the previous night. Someone had the bag, someone else had the wallet. Once a half finished manuscript had found its way to Dwarka before I realised it was missing. It was harder to track the countless cuts and scrapes. And there was always some time that managed to get away.

Why do I lose myself in texts and landscapes? I often find myself in old attics rambling nonsense to myself, jambling over the contents, going over old daguerreotypes and love letters that were never posted.

hanta ta idam pravakshyami guhyam brahma santanam:
yatha ca maranam prapya aatma bhavati gautama

Look (here). I shall explain it to you the mystery of Brahman, the eternal and also how the soul fares, after reaching death, O Gautama.

I keep turning this verse in my head. Sometimes I write it down, so I can be rid of it. But it always keeps coming back. It's the sixth verse from the second section of the Katha Upanishad.

It's followed by the seventh verse:

yonim anye prapadyante sariratvaya dehinah

sthanum anye nusamyanti, yatha karma, yatha shrutam

Some souls enter into a womb of embodiment; others enter stationary objects according to their deeds and according to their thoughts.

If karma determines what we come back as, then I wonder what poets reincarnate into. The verse leaves open some room for the possibility that we could come back as inanimate objects. If so I'd like to come back as a typewriter, in the hands of a talentless writer. This way I could continue writing through him. And he can rest easy in the knowledge that he is an inspired artist. I wonder if the same thing is happening to me, as I type out these words. Who is the spirit in my typewriter that keeps me typing into the late hours of the night?

I'm walking by the river side with staff in hand, slowly turning over the river pebbles with it.

Ginsberg is the yellow butterfly that alights on my staff.

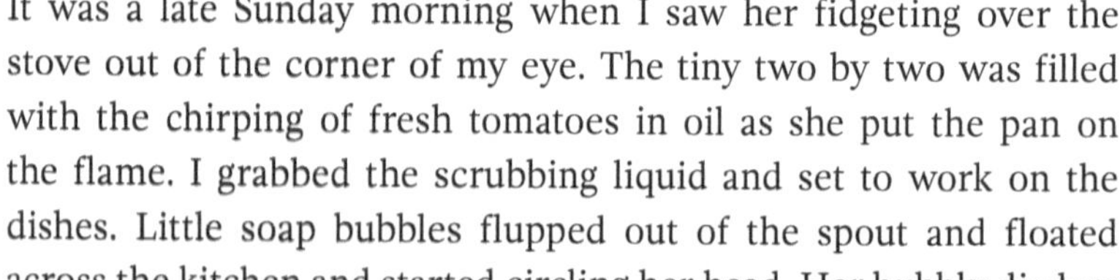

It was a late Sunday morning when I saw her fidgeting over the stove out of the corner of my eye. The tiny two by two was filled with the chirping of fresh tomatoes in oil as she put the pan on the flame. I grabbed the scrubbing liquid and set to work on the dishes. Little soap bubbles flupped out of the spout and floated across the kitchen and started circling her head. Her bubbly diadem came apart as the pearls gently found their way to ground.

Every morning I wake up with the sheets crumpled only on my side of the bed.

The living and the dead both come to be lost in the waters. The river erases the already thin line between these two states of existing. The waters don't discriminate between ash and flesh. To them there is little distinction betwixt living raft and a boat grave. Wood is wood and flesh is flesh. And both in equal parts are unconsummated riverbed wrecks.

Cities and Rivers

How is a city like a river? How is anything like anything? The lowest common denominator is change. We can't step into the same city twice. We can't step into the same river twice. We can't step into the same memory twice. Already in the act of remembering we have changed the memory. It is now tainted with the act of remembering; imbued with the echo of us stupidly sitting in a warm chair as we try to recall the vast open fields and the cold air at the Himalayan gateways.

Glacial waters carry the memory of rock and ice. Black waters carry the remembrance of industry. The rivers inside me, colourless, formless carry the weight of my thoughts and my recollections.

What more truth can I fill these pages with? What thoughts and secret whispers for these blank sheets of paper that are always waiting for pencil scratches and type strikes? The golden hour of the day is now passing and the soft ochre light finds its way around the clouds clashing against the dull sapphire sky. Quetzalcoatl's breath light on the evening eastern wind. Suffering sharpens blades and the outlines of one's character. I am tired now of sharp lines and distinctions. The fuzzy haze of unknowing wisdom calls back to me. And I am tempted to trace my way back to it. It is in not looking that some things are found, or in looking for something else. Like misplaced keys perhaps wisdom can be found when one is looking for neither of them but for a pair of sunglasses. Some truth is hard to find while other is harder to look at even when it resides in our hearts. And so I ask myself:

Do I weep for my father? Or Do I weep the bitter tears of my own loneliness. I feel the poison in my veins waiting to take over. I am guilty. I know. I cry not just for his absence but for another's as well. Even in death I confess I have managed to do yet another injustice to him. My father who went to death peacefully. My father whose own father spews venom now that he's gone. My father whose sister tirelessly works to make a quick buck from his corpse. My father whose son makes him share his memory in his mind. My father whose son now sits alone in a room with junk in his vein and broken dreams in his heart. My father whose son makes him share sentences with him. My father the old tathagata sage of old teeth and tried and tested wisdom of life. My father who sold televisions and dvd players and paper and chemicals and life coated with the perfect happiness of sweet memories and caramel remembrances.

The black gondola rocks softly on the Ganges as it carries away some of my heart with it. On the scales my heart can never be lighter than the feather. But they will both fall equally in vacuum. I am not chasing after a dream. I am not chasing her. I am not running along the river to see it one last time before it crosses the bend and vanishes forever from my sight. I am not.

If there is fear and pain in things ending, then beginnings are the culprit. The tragedy of birth is the red handed shadow that hangs over our lives. Death is the inevitable conclusion. Spring brings about autumn. It is the first shared glance that begets heartbreak and misery. In conception then lies the true calamity. It is they who lead the way to endings. It is their movement that traces out paths in flat circular time.

So many questions go unasked. We never bother looking into the simple mundanities of someone else's life while they are with us. It is only as an aftertaste that we manage to sense a life. And try in vain to recover the flavour of the empty cup.

I spend my days surrounded by greeting cards and gift mugs. Somewhere in these old cassettes and records, somewhere in the old Japanese walkmans and transistor radios, somewhere in old work notebooks that detail building and floor dimensions, there must be something new I can learn about him.

Understanding eludes me at these hours. I shuffle through old files and folders looking for something that isn't there. Chasing abstractions has become a habit that I just can't kick anymore. It is the bane of my waking hours and of my sleeping hours. Living through it is the only remedy I've found. No it is not remedy. Not healing, only a willful suppression of the symptoms. It isn't desirable but nor is it undesirable. It is in the realm of is-ness where all the unescapable facts of our lives dwell.

When I've exhausted myself I stand in the little balcony and watch the wind dance over the leaves over a warm cup of camomile and smile at the stars and the streetlights and maybe even sing to the sleeping dogs.

We were sitting on the banks of the Ganges smoking tea through old clay chillums with black snakes embossed on them with red eyes and a single red jewel on their head. We called out to the other people on the little riverbank beach and they called out to some other people and before we knew it we had music and the night air was thick with the promise of ganja smoke spiralling to the clouds.

As the evening grew heavier people drifted off again in groups of threes and fours, crossing the bridge to get to the other shore and some others off on their way to the upstream ghats.

I am alone on the ghat, on the last ghat on this river of forgetting, on the shores of this river of forgetfulness. I carry secret hopes of losing my memories, my thoughts and even my name to the waters as I breathe in the night.

The cold wind slowly takes away the clouds and leaves me standing under the starry sky. It feels as if someone has taken the dark grounds of the night and mixed them up with small bright burning spots of light, stirred them in together and slowly pressed them out of a coffee press, and then poured the sweet concoction all over the night.

On the ghat across the shore the evening aarti has already started, sending yellow light dancing over the river. I stepped into the river and let the night blue waters cool my feet, slowly sinking into the sand. The floating diyas from the aarti upstream slowly make their way across the bend in the river. Floating balls of fire and light bobbing up and down on the water. I looked up at the stars in the sky and those on the river with open arms and my head thrown back. I feel it slipping away. Everything. My hopes and fears and thoughts and memories and even my dreams. I feel my life slip away into the cold river. And I know if I let myself go, here in Rishikesh the current would bear me all the way to Varanasi, or further still to deltas and then to the ocean.

CHAPTER FOUR

THE LONELY COTTAGE IN THE POLAR WOODS

I dream myself back to the lonely cottage in the polar woods, when I think of Her. The wind is chilly outside. The fog closes her heavy lids over her grey eyes. The liquid moon pours over the Himalayan night.

Sky lights don't shine over the tropic of cancer.

Green-red curtains of absolute pure ecstasy, visible from the suburbs of Canada and Scandinavia, but meant only for the eyes of the solitary travellers in the polar night. What visions await the traveller who ventures out into the void under the stars?

I keep warm on cold swing nights at the dying hearth of these thoughts. The places I visit inside my mind, unfinished poems, half thought out meditations aflame in the hawankund of eternal light at my veranda on starless black liquorice nights.

Writing is a decadent indulgence, isn't it? Putting words on the page – Perhaps thoughts themselves are a borrowed indulgence. I bite my lip as I flip the newspaper to read below the flap. My mouth is filled with the coppery taste of blood. I think I have convinced myself in my heart of hearts that there is something fundamentally twisted about this act of creation.

Is it not better to stop at once? Stop putting ink and graphite to paper. Stop banging needlessly on typewriters. Halt the words from taking form and return them to the sludge of non-meaning. And failing all this, quickly commit to fire what has already been written down or typed up.

How permanent is ink anyway? Old bills, receipts, bus tickets are wiped clean in a few weeks. The ink flies off, and with it the memory of what was there, of what was once an important appointment, of what once was. Photocopied laser ink dallies a bit longer, but it too vanishes. Typewritten ink however, pressed into the very fabric of the paper, outlasts them all. All the same it is still vulnerable to fire.

Words slowly turning to ash take to the wind; Memories turn to ash to dust. If only forgetting was a game as easily played as feeding paper to fire.

I suppose most of our lives share the same significance as old bus tickets; they get us where we need to go, and then disappear of their own accord. We forget the countless journeys, countless but identical in their differences.

Sometimes, I wish I could forget everything, laugh it all away, and watch joyously as the cheap ink flies off the Xerox sheets of my Existence.

The ice cool blue of the Himalayas takes over the landscape. The sky dotted with sparse clouds, little fluffs of bluish white cotton and the mountains a deeper darker more ancient blue. The horizon is painted only with shades of blue.

The wind lightly touches my lips, heavy with memories of forgotten loves, and then flies off just like them. The only one who could understand my desolation was lost somewhere now in the backrooms of my mind.

I bite on a piece of blueberry liquorice as I take it all in.

The landscape races past the bus window, slip-shod brickwall sheds with closed shutters, lonely thatched clay huts, and buildings painted in soft tonal greens, neat indigos, violets and cool light blues.

Across the sky bands of red are breaking out in between the blues. I see them reflected in a small river of clear water that runs over polished stones.

Under the bright noonday sun, the bus follows the straight road, crossing the farms with solitary houses peppered across the rising valley. The unshaped wooden plank doors and slanting roofs are covered in slate roof tiles or grey stone slabs standing vigil over the valley. And after years of elemental damage the sheds that were once sparkling silver are now slowly rusting into a dirty brown. One of the houses has a small mossy concrete staircase in front of it. The staircase begins with the bold intention of going somewhere, but then ends abruptly mid -air. Leading to pure possibility now, what otherwise might have ended up as a dull annexe.

The knotty wooden trees growing out of the rocks, the lonely bamboos on the roadside softly sway in the wind, the corrugated tin on the lonely houses gently pulls on my heart. How can I be nostalgic for a place I have never seen before?

The first willow I see is standing alone in a light brown field, its branches heavy with some unbearable solitude.

We stopped a short distance away from the city. The road was blocked by the Mountain goats and goat herders. We patiently waited for them to move to a by lane further down. Their round heavy horns bobbed in unison against the backdrop of the green tin roofs and dulcet red brick walls.

The driver started the engine and we were on our way again. The outline of the town was slowly taking shape on the horizon. As we entered its bounds, the car had to squeeze through a block of greyed dusty wooden buildings that were half an inch from my face. We made our way through the labyrinth mish mash of the old buildings. Their mossy decaying façades were held together with the vines that weaved in and out of the stones. At every turn, the style of the buildings changed, getting older as we moved closer in towards the center. The driver stopped the car before a narrow cobblestone path and told us, that he couldn't take us any further, and that there were a couple of cheap hotels were a short walk away.

The town was looped in on itself and could be walked around well within the space of half an hour. We started walking the concrete road that was closed unto itself, and like the serpent biting its own tail, had no beginning and no end. I stepped into a new town every time the circle began anew. Slowly but surely the road, the tree impaled house on one corner, the Buddhist temple on the other, were sinking into my soul.

The temple was dedicated to Kalachakra. The walls were adorned with Prayer wheels, and you were supposed to spin the wheels to offer your prayers as you walked around the temple. I stepped in and let my hands trail over the embossed metal.

The evening brought with it strong winds, and the winds brought with them mountain earth in the form of dust. I waked out of the store hands tucked in my jacket and carrying with me books by some of the local poets under my arm. It took a while before I found everyone else huddled together in a corner smoking and debating der zeitgeist and trying to light new cigarettes in the strong wind which was making them go out too quickly. The trees were dangerously close to being unrooted and taking off with the wind.

After some time we stepped inside a café to take shelter from the dust and spent the night drinking warm tea and laughing over old embarrassments as the winds howled outside.

Instead of going back to our rooms, we decided to go to the roof and lie down by the solar panels. The concrete was cold, but the wind was soft and carried indescribable warmth with it. The stars were lowered over the valley like a mosquito net and for the first time in my life I understood why planetariums were constructed the way they were. I lied down on my concrete bed and watched the starlight filter through the air and come to me.

Whenever I've looked at the night sky, I've only ever seen solitary stars scattered through the void and they've always made me melancholy. I feel the crushing weight of their uncountable beauty bearing down on me every time I raise my head to look at them.

As the night wore on the sounds of our sneezes rang out in the valley. And when the last drop of Tea was gone we decided to go back to our rooms. I crashed on my mattress and was whisked off to the polar woods.

Dreamscape

The cottage stands on the slopes of a snowclad peak; an eagle's solitary eyrie for two. She's always there, reading by the fireplace in the polar night. Her hair tied up in a bun.

I don't quite remember when the cottage moved from the Austrian Alps to the Lower Himalayas in the antipodes of my sleeping mind. It brought the northern lights with it, when it did.

Her hand was resting on the armchair when I walked in. She was looking at it with the infinite curiosity of a child, slowly moving it and watching the shadows change through the space between her fingers.

"I'm sorry that I didn't show up last time", I said. I took off my coat and gently placed it on the stool next to the door, taking care to not disturb the silence that was draped over the room.

"Where were you this time" she asked, slowly shifting her hand a little.

"I was stuck in a railway station somewhere. The trains slid in and left the platform like clockwork, but I couldn't get on one, no matter what I tried. So I sat down and watched them leave one after the other"

She moved her hand in a full circle, twisting her wrist now one way, and now the other, contemplating the meaning of my dream. I cleared out the books from the other sofa, and sat down facing her. The rhythmic cracking of the fireplace sent out waves of drowsiness through the room.

Suddenly struck by some inspiration, she sat upright, crossing one leg over the other in one swift motion.

"We could always meet each other on a train station, if that's what you'd prefer."

"No. No, this place suits me just fine." I blurted out. "Things are fine the way they are"

"Of course you think that when I am the one who has to wait for hours on end, when you get lost on your way here." I could sense her growing exasperation.

"I know. I am sorry. I'll be here on time next time"

"Oh but you always say that"

"That I do" I said, rummaging around for the cigarettes in my pockets, remembering that they were in the coat; I gave up on them and directed my attentionto her instead.

She had picked up her reading glasses and was turning them over in her hands.

"What does this place look like to you now?"

"Oh, it's still a cottage for me"

"Where?", she asked sensing my evasion.

"In the lower Himalayas somewhere, I can't remember where" I lied.

"Have you ever been there?"

"I'm sure I must have. And what is this place to you?"

"It's an old manor in the Balkans somewhere, I'm not sure where either." She placed her elbow on the armrest, resting her face on her palm. Her brows knit together, troubled at the realisation of her exact whereabouts, or lack thereof.

"I'm sure you'll remember when you wake up", I consoled her picking up the string of her unsaid thoughts.

"It's not an issue really. I have a better memory than you."

"I remembered you a little last time"

"We both know that's a lie"

"There might be some truth in there so be a little kind"

"When you do me the kindness of remembering me after you've woken up, that is the day you ask for my kindness"

She got up and started pacing about the room; her feet sounding softly over the wood boards, disappearing shortly over the carpet, and reappearing on the other side.

"Do you remember the words at least?"

"Dreamless sleep falls over the gentle night"

I walked over and took her by the arm. I could see the green blue flames dancing in her eyes. She grabbed me by my jacket, crushing the fabric in her hands, and lifting herself on her tiptoes, locked her lips with mine. We clawed at each other filled with the longing of children who had been cheated out of something that was promised them.

She broke off and pushed me away.

"Now go wake up. But remember this."

"I will"

"You never do"

"I never do"

"You never do", and with that she vanished from the room; her afterimage still hovering over the space that she had left behind her.

I sat down in her seat by the fireplace, picked up the book she'd been reading, and let my eyes run over the words, slowly moving my tongue over my lips that tasted of her for several hours.

It was time for the climb. We readied our gear and started up the trail. The weather was fickle, but soothing in its changes. After about two or three kilometres, we stopped hearing any human noises but our own. The buzz of street lamps was replaced by the actual buzzing of bees and other insects and in the air you could hear their tiny wings flapping to the beat.

*

A red butterfly flew to the rhododendrons
A yellow butterfly passes by
Impelling me up the mountain rock
The rush of the waterfall rings out in the valley
The pitter patter of the rain blends in

*

I sit in an alcove formed by the rocks
Seeking refuge from the pour
The music of the waterfall reverberates
Inside my private sanctuary
Dark and grey, On grey stones

*

An eagle glides across the peaks storm clouds roar out
I cool my feet in the white froth of the waterfall
The cold sting of the water makes me hop out
Shivering like an ungraceful frog
The white sheepdog watching me
Nods its head thoughtfully
And then trots over the river swift and surefoot
A bodhisattva in his own right

I sat down on a boulder on the trail, under the mountain sun with Johnny the dog, his black fur shining brightly against the snow. The mountain dogs had followed us along the snowy trail, all-knowing and wise in the ways of the Himalayas and lapping up food from our hands.

The air is intoxicating and I didn't feel the slightest craving for a smoke or a drink. The sun hot on our backs made us take off our jackets and the sun won once again as in Aesop's fable. We tied our jackets around our waists as the wind frowned.

I walk over to this beautiful cherry tree and start admiring its branches. I started pulling on one of the lower ones, until it eventually gave way and broke off in my hands. I began peeling off the bark as we continued up the trail. And slowly the white skin of the branch started shining as brightly as the Himalayan snow.

I borrowed a knife from a friend and used its blunt end to smoothen out the branch. Over the next two hours, I slowly fashioned it into a staff. The snow appeared in small patches out of nowhere. And as we trudged on, the patches started getting larger and larger, until it became quite impossible to go any further without traversing through snow.

At this point most of the first timers wanted to turn back and weren't sure they could make it to the top. It took a lot of cajoling and pleading to bring them around. I was hooked by this point and had to see the summit after coming all this way.

I am not one
    A different me breathes in
    The cold sharp air
    The mount reminds me
    Of my multitudes
    *

    The hawk in the sky
    Mindfully eyes
    The yellow butterfly
    My yellow friend alights on my staff
    Resting its wings
    Before flying off
    The hawk snatches her in his beak

And slowly glides down the valley

I had learned from one of the locals downhill that the rhododendrons were made into chutney and tasted brilliant right off the tree. I plucked a few bunches and stuffed them into my pockets greedily. The sweet sour taste of the flower rolled right of my tongue tasting like Zen. It took us some time to find clean snow that wasn't mixed in with the mud. As soon as I found some, I rolled it into an ice ball and bit into it and it rang out with a wide crunch crush of absolute ecstatic freshness.

*

The ice ball fresh on my tongue
The sweet-sour of the bransa blends in
With the Himalayan cool
Like a mountain goat
My feet unthinking, lead the way.

The act of digging my shoes into the ice to keep from going over the edge clears my mind. I saved a lot of energy by using the footholds that were predug into the snow. Every time the trail got a little trickier I planted my staff deep into the snow and the mud and used it to pivot around the turns and the ends.

The melting snow flowed down the mountain side in tiny rivulets. And every once in a while it would pool in into little rock basins, I cupped it into my hands and schlepped it

around in my mouth before finally gulping it down.

We reached the peak in five hours. I laid my eyes on the lower Himalayas that stretch out from where I was to Nepal and then Tibet and onto China. Everyone pulled out their cameras pretty quickly, which I took as my cue to leave and seek out some well-earned solitude in the lap of the Himalayas.

I found a little decline that lead to a small flat landing laden with snow. Far away from the commotion everyone was stirring up on the other side. I threw myself back on the bed of snow. The snow cold on my back, the mountain sun daggering bright on my eyes; both vying for my attention. The clouds crawling across the sky and the sun hiding behind them. I cherish this gift of the Himalayas as she coaxes me back into her folds.

After hours of silence, or minutes, but passing with the weight of hours, I opened my eyes and looked at the mountain in front of me, and saw in its edifice shapes and signs spelled out in the rock and ice. I took out my notebook and recorded the visions:

Two Visions
A warrior poised to throw his spear, a bat flying around his head.
A wolf with broken legs howling at the silent moon.

Yellow butterflies have faded out
    In the land of the white butterflies
    I watch one fly against the canvas
    Of the mountain rock
    My soul flies away with it

*

Gudang garam
Acridly sweet on my tongue
My pencil scratches paper in the ice cool
The caw caw of the crow rings out in the silence
The sun shines bright again, but softer now

The shy peaks are hiding in the clouds
    The pines watch me stoically as I wait for their approval
    The crow perched on the leafless tree shakes his head in disapproval
    And flies off into the valley
    I drink the ice in little sips of tea patience

And ask myself
Did Zarathustra slip on his way back down from the mountain?

*

The dogs lap up biscuits from my hands at Triund
I chant OM into the valley
My eyes closed
The crows are silent now

*

I trust my staff on snow
More than I trust people
The three legged man
In the noon of his life
Goes down the evening mount

We started down the mountain, taking a different route, and much to our surprise found men there digging in the snow with pick axes. We asked them what they were up to, and they told us about the evershifting snow and how there was a shop buried under there and how the little bulb was still on inside somewhere. The owner was worried about the electric bill and wanted to get to the off switch pronto. The invisible hand of the electric department instils greater fear in the hearts of the same men, who slide straight across the mountain snow with nothing but their climbing shoes.

Nightmare

I sit for hours on my bed, slowly watching myself burn out like a tallow candle. The flame starts slowly on the fingertips of my left hand, and moves further once it has eaten its way to the bone. I don't feel any pain as I watch my bony hand, held together by some preternatural force; preserving its transcendental handness, despite there not being much of it left.

With idle curiosity I sit and watch the fire eat away at my flesh for hours on end.

The first thing that comes to my mind when I think of the Himalayas is not the snow or the air; it's the old worn out gaming arcades. Small rooms filled with racing and shooter games from the early nineties. Claw machines rigged to fail seventy percent of the time. There's nothing quite like them. I remember when I was a kid, how my father would stay with me for hours, shelling out hundreds on some fps game, so I could complete it before leaving the next morning. Sometimes I wonder if the kids who die from falling off from the mountains, come back to the arcades at night.

Hiding inside the folds of the mountains, are so many old cemeteries, holding the bones of people who have no people to remember them. I read their epitaphs as we make our way down. They're embossed on stone scrolls, or open books of stones. There are some bible verses and sometimes poems from poets who were popular in their times. But now are lost to the indifference of passing time. It is fitting perhaps, to have forgotten words for forgotten people. Here's something we all share: The certainty of being forgotten after enough time passes, and failing that the certainty of there not being anyone left to do the remembering.

The population of these hills never changes. The cities might be flooded with visitors at times. But there aren't many who stay here forever. And on the rare occasion someone does, a local leaves for the metropoles in search of a better life. The population never changes. If I can't step in the same river twice, and if I can't step in the same city twice, then it is only natural that I can't trek across the same mountain twice. Perhaps that is why so many people get lost in the ranges and never find their way back home.

L' Appel du Vide

It will be quite a while before I will be able to see the sun set over the Himalayas. The café I'm in right now is a glass box suspended a little over the hill side and I can see the sky under my feet. Things always call out to us; even the absence of all things has its own mating call. I have always found it in me to follow what calls out to me, oceans, sands, hills, cities, and yet here is a deafening howl that registers deeper than all others, a call that I can't heed. There isn't enough reason to take the leap. There isn't enough faith to take it either. What Metaphysical acrobatics can justify the turn from non-meaning to meaning.

The search for meaning is not a leap. It isn't the confluence of two eternally perpetuating halves, or eternally recurring time. The search for meaning is the search for trees in the forest; a search for patterns that emerge out of their arrangement. The best place to hide a tree is in the forest, to hide a building; a city, and to hide the person; a crowd.

It is difficult to gain perspective from the forest floor, and impossible to glean anything from the sky, the canopy hides the trees from would be gods. The best view of things is gained from a medium height, and it is upon us to expert the art of climbing trees. And then climb down just as swiftly, and devote our lives to this endless forest; to the eternal jungle of repeating signs. We have managed to sufficiently stamp out what little there was in us, of the nomadic disposition, and often find ourselves sitting alone in clearings of our own creation; burning the timber, to keep warm as the soot laced clearing grows larger and larger around us. The only antidote to this is an endless wandering, an endless wandering that settles the soul with its lack of stillness, the equilibrium of unbalance in the search of unattainable meaning.

The mad king wanders the forests writing poetry.

CHAPTER FIVE

SKY ISLAND ABOVE THE OCEANS OF EUROPA

I remember the sun setting on my island above the oceans of Europa.

The warmth of the sun weans away as the last rays trickle over my neck and then the horizon.

Sometimes, it turns in upon itself and vanishes altogether. I'm left inverted, in the sky with the ice above my head and the stars beneath my feat. My insides are unsettled; I walk around my private heaven to ease the nausea. I wander the empty expanse, the clouds under my feet as I watch the stars trace their way across the sky.

I look up and see the frozen oceans, and wonder what the fish are doing miles beneath the ice. I look at the stars and wonder how many of them must already be dead.

I feel at home.

The Tin Can Bodhisattva

A homeless man is meditating in the heart of the city. He's sitting cross legged like the yogis of old on a pile of ancient mouldy blankets, one on top of the other. The blankets have failed to preserve their individuality and are one more or less now. The bodhisattva is surrounded by cans of tin, of aluminium, and even of polyvinyl chloride. The cans are open at the top, waiting to collect the waters of some invisible rain. Is he then the bodhisattva of tin cans, or of empty tins?

Some mornings when the sky is covered in shades of azure and egyptian, I take my time to step outside and water the aloe vera plants on the balcony. I lose myself in the simple act of pouring water on the mud and watching it slowly drink it in. My thoughts are always cut short with the arrival of the paperboy. The morning newspaper flies over my head and strikes against the various objects kept outside. If the paperboy was born in a different time and in a different place, with that arm he'd make a good pitcher.

Years change like seasons and in other rooms other voices are singing to each other while I sit alone nursing my own melancholy. I find my mind flitting now to things, now to places and kings and people past and present. All things are equal and chaos the highest form of order.

The passage of time fails to heal wounds but makes it a social necessity to hide them deep inside our sleeves. No one wants to hear of an old tragedy as if it happened yesterday or even today as I was adding sugar to my morning coffee. It is in bad taste to renew in the social memory of that which they've forgotten long ago.

My city is an acronym covered in trees. It is a city without memory. It is a city of malls and gutters and trees. The black death waters of Hindon to the north and the white death waters of the Yamuna to the south. Noida has no memory because it has no history.

People live here. They haunt the streets. They fall in love and do their taxes in this city. They walk around the floodlit parks and stroll across the vast malls drowning in the silence of distant store announcements. It's easy to forget in a city that's all about that retail lifestyle.

The highway and the metro are at level with my roof. At night cars fly across the horizon and trains lazily pull up into the dully lit platform in the distance. If I try hard I can see the outlines of my high school in the distance. Wherever I have been, whatever I have seen, nothing changes the fact that a large majority of my life has been spent within this little circle of buildings and highways and empty development lots.

And the city is right there with me; unchanging. A city circling the same ideas of what life is and what it should be. There is some new non-change every other month that has the people gazing in dead amazement at the city's streets. Some new mall or parking lot opens up to the adulation and admiration of this city. Life becomes marginally easier, and the people marginally more complacent.

Pachisi

Usually when I cut class as a kid, I ended up walking around the city. Places I'd usually pass by in a car, I could see come to life as I meandered around the streets. I remember spending hours watching the idle rickshaw pullers play the street potters at Pachisi. They drew the board on the cracked sidewalk with chalk, and if there was no chalk around then in red brick shards. Little Seep shells raced across the improvised game board, as small rocks substituted for dice. Now when I walk along those same roads everyone is glued to their touch screens.

I have seen the town filled with friends and family and future loves. I have seen the city after everyone, friends, and family had left. I have seen the shadows of past loves hanging over the sky. I have slept through the night and through the afternoons. I have lived through unending afternoons and sleepless nights. If there was a lesson in all this life, I seem to have missed it.

To what end do I wander the streets of this town, are there any ends to a Flâneur's maunderings. I paint stories for the people passing me by on the streets. I have found solitude in crowds and in the company of friends; I've only ever found loneliness. My solitude is peopled, and my isolation crowded.

There is greater comfort at times in striking a conversation with a stranger that you know you'll never see again, than with a friend or a lover you've known for years.

I am not looking for the light at the end of the tunnel. I am looking for the firefly at the end of the abyss. I am the thought that echoes back to me, and I am the abyss that absorbs all sound and light.

I'm surrounded by great marvels of suburban architecture. The dusty boulevards and avenues with asbestos and construction sand caking the street in a thin frosting of grey. Empty eyeless skyscrapers without windows or entirely covered in glass curtains eerily reflecting the light from the passing automobiles. I see you sleeping on the sidewalk on the doorsteps of this soulless glass and concrete. I see me sleeping on the sidewalk. I see all of us sleeping on the sidewalks.

Vacant landscape

Small changes inside empty malls catch my attention — the clicking of heels on the marble floors, jibber jabber drivel conversations in the distance, the sound of cash registers and store announcements mixed in with the largely vacant malls. Every visit to this mausoleum is a mallsoft album in itself.

I'm not sitting in a dead mall. There is still life in it, but the people are sloughing away in their far off offices in Dwarka and Gurgaon and who knows where else. The empty sounds register themselves on the blank tape recorder playing in the recesses of my soul. Only bored housewives, sad old men and teenagers in love people it the mall at these hours. I watch them trace out their blurry lives for a few hours. They too are a part of my world; a part that is never remembered but only ever recalled in a vague hazy recollection of something that happened, but was of no consequence.

It used to be malls were built and then they died, but now in the far reaches of Greater Noida new malls are built dead on arrival. I've spent many hours walking the empty corridors looking at the vacant lots of glass and uncovered concrete and open electrical wiring climbing across the spaces. Hours enveloped in the faint smell of stale coffee and cleaning agents that waft over the southern end of the malls and find their way northward.

Sometimes entire basements are carved out for a winter wonderland adventure that never gets built. Other times indoor gondolas sail across sickly blue water channels that snake across the mall. There are more balustrades and pointless bridges and alleyways and staircases inside them to house a small town. I see the emptiness in the polished marble. I see starving families haunting the empty shops and basements.

I bought a new box of cake matches yesterday. They changed the design on the back. Now it's a softened ochre yellow and brick red separated by the word 'Cake Matches.' I think the lettering is something one would see on an old theatre in L.A. that was built in the 70s, the neon broken down and dusty now. This match box belongs to the bedside of a mad broke writer banging on his second hand underwood nameless in the sixties, nameless in the seventies.

And yet it is here, and now in my hands, as I light my cigarette with it and casually toss it across the desk, nameless.

Why are supermarkets always in basements underground, sometimes even two or three floors below the sunlight—Floodlights, Floodlights, Floodlights— Aisles of produce and fruits for our starving muddy stomachs. I stroll around the bright floodlit miles of waxed flooring, changing direction on whim with no more than two or three things in my cart. Who listens to the garbled store announcements, who buys the cheese and jalapeño dips on promotion after tasting it for free. I wonder how many supermarkets I would need to visit in a day to fill my stomach solely on the promotional grub. The floodlights in supermarkets intrusive as the floodlights in a prison, what interrogations do they foreshadow.

I would glide around the shopping cart if one of the wheels wasn't damaged. I wonder if they damage them on purpose. To keep people from sailing across the neatly waxed floors as they hoard a months' worth of grocery.

Rainy Landscape

Weekly markets travel across the face of the city like old nomads who after years of wandering have tired of exploring new places but can't give up their nature either, and so have settled for the compromise of routine. The markets are always open. Even if I don't know where the vendors are on some given day, I can rest easy with the certainty that every night somewhere under the roof of this city the vendors are again repacking their wares for the new day.

There are incalculable thingamajigs for sale in the market. All sorts of oils and spices and stationary and clothes and all things imaginable under the sun for bargain prices that get lower and lower as the moon climbs higher in the starless skies.

In the cloudburst months sudden rainfall clears out the bustling bazars. The public scurries off back into their warm two by twos or three by threes leaving behind the few insightful individuals who had put away secret umbrellas into the folds of their existence — and a few others who aren't afraid of their souls growing a little damp from the rain. The shops grow turtle shells of yellow, blue and white tarp supported by bamboo skeletons. The tarmac a perfect mirror that reflects back the neon blue, violet indigo and sometimes clean white light. Lonesome cars send headlight yellow orbs sailing across the asphalt mirror.

The air, pure now with the scent of rain lightly falling takes over my senses. And for a few minutes I am one of the nameless others who hide somewhere in my soul.

It's a wonder people still write to each other. It's a greater wonder still that people write to me. I never throw out letters— the memories of old flames and new, of thunderstorms and light drizzles, all preserved in ink and paper.

I have all sorts of letters, some of them written in a rush on torn pieces of ruled or blank paper from notebooks or diaries or journals. Others planned for months with a beautifully written opening, middle and an end on cream letter stock or craft paper. And a few with salutations and a few sentences explaining why even after weeks she couldn't come up with anything and has had to leave the letter blank.

I don't read them often, or at all. They have power not because of what they say, but simply as objects that one owns and has at hand, even if they are not of use.

Mag Rath: Tales of the forest
The mad king wanders the forests writing poetry. From glen to glen, wherever his derangement takes him, pausing only to rest on the branches of Yews scattered through the land. At every clearing

and brook he pauses to compose verses, weaving in the land around him into meter and rhyme and similes and metaphors. The king wandered for seven years as a mad man — never at peace, with demons and things biting and slashing at his heels, real or of his own imagining. In moments of perfect clarity he looked around and saw the madness of the world, saw his own helplessness in the face of it all.

How then is the poet thrown into the forests of concrete and glass any different from the banished king of Dal Araide? Aren't the rocky clefts of wilderness as hard as the corner of the padlocked cells? There is no glen for the madmen in this city. I remember the mad men were sequestered off to an asylum, but I've forgotten where the asylum is.

The world has always conspired to pass me by. And for years, through the changing seasons I've tried to run after it, to catch the last compartment of a train that is always leaving. Sometimes a kind stranger extends a hand and pulls me in. Othertimes I take the leap, but I've always made it.

And then I gave it up. I left the station and walked as far from the mania as my feet would take me. I have left it, but it hasn't left me. Even now as I spend my days watching people go about their lives, a part of me wants to go and check if the train has left or if there's still a chance of getting on. I am tired of waking up in the middle of the night panicking over things that are already so far in the past that they can find no other way to torment me but in my dreams.

In my solitude and in the act of turning the present into memories, I have understood the impossibility of ever understanding someone with all their imperfections and the thousand facets of their soul intact. It isn't as easy to press a button and instantly press out Polaroids of the spirit.

And this understanding was followed swiftly by the naiveté that made me want to try in the first place. I am quite content now to simply brush my elbow against something that is a rough approximation of the person I see with my eyes— the image which in turn itself is another approximation.

I see an endless city. A city that covers an entire planet, that grows over the land and the ocean like a fecund tumour begetting more tumours. It belches its gunk into the oceans and injects it into the land. We are the last humans, the last animals peopling this metropolis bathed in the glow of giant neon signs that orbit us in the sky.

There are no more prairies to drive across, and no ponds left to mull over, only the city. The patterns repeat, same windows glower down on the bums peeing in the streets, identical doors shut in the face of pamphleteers, the same indistinguishable eyes go about their day without a sideway glance to the dispossessed. Sad eyes that don't look for each other. Grey eyes aimlessly darting over things never taking anything in.

The city is destiny carved in granite and cement and in bleeding red bricks.

In the mire of existence the only lasting solace a person can find is inside themselves. There is great hope and warmth in love and in lovers, but the true disquietude within can only be conquered from within. In the broad empty expanses of one's consciousness there is a silence that can never be found in the world of people and things. It is our greatest source of misfortune that therein also dwells a pandemonium unmatched.

Perhaps we would live in a more fulfilled world if we spent more time navigating the far recesses of our own selves.

I say this as the offhanded statement of a simple fact and nothing more. This isn't an expression of some secret hope for the individual or for the many gnats that people this universe. I am not a believer in the humanist faith and yet I don't feel comfortable around anyone who isn't a believer in this convoluted doctrine. There are people who are hunched over old tomes of poetry in dusty libraries and their hearts are bursting with love for humans and humanity. Melodies and ballads flow through their beings as they think of the common blood and marrow of the citizenry. I try to keep as far away from these characters as I can. For they are characters; Pastiches discarded by novelists and left to wander the shit and piss soaked streets of the world. And remember when you run across them in the streets be kind to them they are your sisters and your brothers and your fathers and your mothers.

The ocean is the sky and the vast empty universe is ebbing under my feet. The only thing I can hope for is a long drunken rest on the shores of my island as the tides bring in and take back liquid sunshine from faraway stars.

There is no void even emptiness is filled with itself. And if I run into someone in the emptiness of my paradise is that someone not me. Both of us are lost in the empty but never vacant, green palm tree coconut Valhalla halls of the mind. I want to sleep dreamless silent sleeps. I want to forget what forgetting is. I don't want to look at the broken buildings, hardened people and the empty flag poles anymore. I promise I will love the depths of your heart for they are the depths of my heart. In the name of the common core of vile selfishness and boundless love that blossoms in all our souls, I proclaim my innocence. And so I proclaim your innocence.

I ask for no hymns or soft chants. I ask for textures and tones stretched to the horizon repeating the same ambient message in time. It is not everywhere that I have freedom but I feel something like it when I rest my weary head on her breasts or when she's curled up in my lap like a bird with broken wings. I don't have any hopes for eternity. I have eternal hopes of the present. And there are times when as I am strolling across my island my sad feet can't tell the grass from the astroturf, and all I can do is sit and watch the uncountable grassblades of cellulose or plastic sway in the wind. The same wind as it caresses my face and ruffles my hair, reassures me that there is something outside of me and my memories.

Bisrakh: Howl of the Asuras

The Demon King is still mourned in the city. With the movement of the moon and the passing of another year it is that time again. I see him go up in fire from my terrace, fireworks bright in the soot laced skies. A little further east, nestled in a thicket of ashokas and banyans there is Bisrakh — of sombre prayers and diyas, in solemn remembrance of the king's passing — a village with distinct memory and history, all of its own.

Legends differ as to why he was called Dashaanan. Was it because of his knowledge of the six Shastras and the four Vedas or because of his mastery of all ten human emotions? He was by all means a complete man. A tragic figure on par with Hercules or perhaps Oedipus serves a better comparison. Few remember him as an author, fewer still as a poet. History and Mythology are rife with biases that help make it become more palatable to a certain kind of mind. A mind that sees and remembers but does not understand, a mind that is agreeable to dogma and to reason insofar it doesn't have to strain itself beyond a certain threshold. A mind attuned to the isness of the status quo.

There are many howls in history and out of the history that demand to be heard. Howls that permeate our waking hours and ask us to look at them, to think about them, to answer their unanswerable questions, to look into their hard eyes as we fumble around our attics looking for words, helpless in the face of simple truths, cold and shivering and mute despite all the books that we carry around in our heart.

Around the temple dogs with tikas were milling around the door watching the passers-by with lazy eyes. The sadhu inside told me that everyone is in mourning now in their homes but come morning it's the same song and dance again.

The King will see fire for years to come. But sometimes I look at the world from my balcony and my wistful heart hopes for a time when he won't have to.

As I look at the apartment buildings from my terrace or from the windows of the metro moving through the city I am overwhelmed by a feeling of nausea. All taste has been avoided in the architecture and in interior design. The ugly façades splotched with the blackness of damp or sometimes left unpainted in dull grey monotones. The ugliness isn't helped by the illegal constructions of the residents who break out outer walls to extend their houses over the ledges for a few extra inches of space.

The complexes themselves are arranged jaggedly in sectors that are numbered by way of accidental toss of dice. The only foresight that I have managed to discern in the construction of my metropolis is the absence of the number thirteen in floors and bungalows and most prominently in the omission of an entire sector. This and other monuments to superstition and old wars lie scattered around old bends hidden away by thick lush grass.

My mind makes bizarre noises as it gyrates under the strain of the world. Around me ghosts glide on by to their haunts in the countless damp flats waiting for the flat sunshine that will come with the morning.

Nightfall—floating orange orbs in the cascading velvet of the night.

All thoughts dissolve as I feel the breath of a strange woman on my skin.

What is it about loneliness that drives us to create endless libraries and cottages and ghats and hotels and even imaginary islands over ice moons of the mind. Why do people walk their souls through the streets crying from loneliness? What lurks in the depths of the collective murk of solitude, of solace, of loneliness and even saudade?

Silent watchers under a tarpaulin of yellow sit together and watch a man pollute an easel for hours while silent music plays on in their heads. Let it then be recorded in heaven's unchangeable heart that I turned my head away, and looked at the watchers watching— if only for a brief instant.

For a few minutes tonight everyone turned off the lights and I could see a thousand stars from my window- open now to the world. Wispy clouds put there in small lazy brush strokes, silently crossing the skies — weary travellers — the red and the yellow of the far away night lamps colouring the horizon in tonal reds shifting into midnight blues. Whose loneliness does the wind carry to me now, as I burden it with my tired sighs.

It is a different thing then to feel lost and out of place — even in dark nights there are things to be said and remembered and sometimes spoken out loud into the darkness...

Olive is the color of my sleepwalking. Life is but a few moments of consciousness, scattered fireworks punctuated with long somnolent interludes. Other colours are muted and swept up under thick woollen carpets. It is easy to forget about them over time. It is easy to forget about a lot of things if you let them be; victims of my casual neglect. While it is child's play to forget them, it is impossible to forget that I have forgotten them. There are winds gnawing at the roof of my mind, frustrated at having being forgotten, displeased at the elaborate fenestrations and the barriers that keep them out.

If you can live with that racket in your head then it is okay to forget about the other colours. In my experience sooner or later, the din becomes intolerable even to the most seasoned misanthrope.

There is always the possibility of friends and of loves. And when friends leave and love fades, green overtakes the landscape again. It must then appear to be a futile exercise to look for the other colours- elusive and hiding- expedient to paint everything green, for there are countless shades to that one color itself - Mint and emerald and moss and fern and jungle and jade and lime & lemonade. A world in green leaves and trees and the wind green with melancholy. It is calming to think of the world made so. There is undeniable harmony in isolation, in lonesome meditation removed from the blue planet, in lush gardens of green on ice white moons.

But then again too much harmony is calamitous to life, monotones are always sterile. It is easy to get sick of green. Green is nausea. Green is nauseating. And every leaf can be looked at only for so long. Soon the heart pines after red letterboxes and silver grey bicycles that ring out in light summer mornings. There is great value in the chase of short-lived pleasures. And sometimes a moment of ephemeral prismatic despair is more desirable than an eternity of calm monotone greens.

And there were continents that swallowed other continents that remerged as mountains or stayed hidden away in the ocean — at times sulking under the tiny islands scattered about the blue Indian Ocean. And things that were written on the ocean floor were lost to water and time.

Trishanku's Empty Heaven

The gods condemned Trishanku to spend an eternity in his own upturned heaven. He is the only inhabitant of his heaven; a man neither of this world nor of the next. His exile is in part self-imposed and as such he is responsible for his isolation inasmuch as the gods.

If the Ramayana is to be taken at its word, Trishanku was once a noble King. In the line of the Suryavanshis, a long time before Dashratha and his sons lived there was Satyavrata. A noble king, Satyavrata having fulfilled his duties in this realm wished to ascend to the next. But Satyavrata was for the lack of a better word a Monoist. He felt that he could not part with his body and wished to take it with him to heaven. This wasn't acceptable to the Dualists around him. When he made his request to Vashishtha, He was rebuked and sent away. Satyavrata then sought out Vashishtha's son Shakti. Shakti could not however grant what his father had denied and asked the king to leave.

Satyavrata coolly told him, that he will just look for someone else who is willing to assist him in his endeavours. Enraged at this Shakti cursed him to be a Chandala and to bear the name Trishanku.

An outcast now, Trishanku aimlessly wandered the wilderness. Vishwamitra, Vashishtha's rival found him and moved by his tale decided to help him out. The Sage started lifting Trishanku to Heaven while Indra, King of the Devas, fearful for his throne started working against him. Indra could not permit Trishanku into Heaven, and Vishwamitra refused to renege on his promise. Finally, a compromise was reached and a new heaven was created for the King. And the king had to dwell in it upside down so as to not challenge Indra's authority.

What good is this eternity? How long before one starts questioning the other world that had once existed and is now nothing but the stuff of memories. Memories that could have been lies fed to us by someone else. I don't see how anyone can bear such a fate and not eventually fall into the deep uncertain pit of solipsism.

To think of serene mountains and dark nights with clear stars shining over the city skyline, only to be able to return to the blind chase, reinvigorated. To love trees for their shade and not much more – for that is all they are good for to the weary.

To haggle after the price of orchids and use Zen wisdom to maximise productivity in invasively lit cubicles – for that is all they are good for to the unoriginal mushrooms of routine. It would suit them if with a dimmer they could dim spring and brighten up autumn.

To falsely convince the heart that it wants not this but that, that which has coin and the promise of measly riches – ikigai madness with cherry blossom petals pulled over the eyes. In my most disturbing day dream, at the back of my head I have sprouted the keys of a cash register and I can feel invisible fingers drawing up the balance of my life and the change to

be tendered.

To forget someone in life only to remember them in death – do we only wish to talk to silent ghosts and absentees who can't defend themselves, woven into the ever changing tapestry of our memories.

To remember that which is better forgotten – balance sheets tucked away, holding to account grudges and favours and even love, what is owed and what was lent, lent out and not given without any expectations. The silent arithmetic recorded by mute bookkeepers.

To lose a love not because it wasn't love but because it was – a life spent crystallising memories and running away from the real and into abstractions' empty embrace.

I dream of all the friends who have left me and who I have left, and countless others who were bystanders but might have been something more and in my dreams there is no strife between them or between them and me. I dream of cardboard cut outs with painted faces, stiller than any still life and uglier than the paint as it runs down the dirty canvas.

The rain on my awning—beats of the silent night. The same slanting rain falls on my clothes drying outside and on the pile of old newspapers that the ragman should have come to collect last wednesday. And I sit here friendless alone in the night scribbling on a piece of paper under the light of the sickle moon.

What colours did you see when you flew to the orient. What shapes do you see from your window open at Algonquian cemeteries? You have your secret pleasures of the soul and I have mine. The distance has never had any meaning. It is tiring to peep in through eyelid jalousie windows of the soul. You don't need to pretend anymore. The place we live in matters little when the distance is inscribed in our souls. Sometimes I feel the pull of spooky action at a distance nudging at my shoulder when you think of me, but I quickly shrug it off.

I am the ghost that haunts eternally your childhood home – White Shrouded Spectre.

Our lady of solitude, I have words for you. Unkind words. Sharp knifed words. Base belches of indigestible hate. Scandalous turns of phrase that would keep you up in the night. Debased utterances solely designed to scathe your soul. With an astounded eye I watch you move through the world, your tricks and wiles trailing behind your evening gown.

My thoughts fly back to my toe crossed lover faraway, stranded on a red sanded plateau beyond my reach— four seasons in a day, every day, years passing in the minute hand of the clock.

I sit on the edge of the island, my feet dangling in the air. The sole river of the island pours into the air, dispersing into little droplets after a little while, raining down on the ice below. Puddles filled with the sky. The other moons fly in and out of view at times. Where do I go from here? If there is meaning to be found in the pursuit of one's self, where does one go after one has found it. Must we not settle into a waking somnolence and simply look at the things around us as they are. Is my restlessness a sign of something lost? The big dipper thoughtfully scratches its head at my questions.

What would make me happy now? Coffee, Cheese, Bread and maybe half a fish head –something drawn out of chance, as arbitrary as my shifting gaze through the constellations.

What business do I have with this moon? What business do I have with the sand coarse under my hands and the shadow of towering palm leaves hanging over the night.

What do the clouds moving over the icescape and passing through my fingertips have to do with me, sitting alone on this island now, on coarse sand under palm shadow with legs dangling over the edge, swinging in the wind.

The rain splashed earth holds within it a million kulhads. The rain sweet on my lips in early fall or late monsoon. The rain falling on ugly houses and vacant parking lots. The rain ringing out in empty malls. The rain turning gargantuan foundations for hopeless buildings into muddy landfills. The rain overflowing the gutters. The rain stopping at the concrete and the asphalt never reaching the soil. The rain drizzling gently now, on my home.

My acronym city deserves all the uncharitable words in my lexicon and those not in it. But for all its flaws it is home. Love sleeps in these houses and walks the empty malls holding hands. Men pour their sweat and blood into the foundations. And the roots of the banyans stretch into the gutters. Memories walk the streets and strange ideas are standing around the corner smoking. And sometimes I even stumble across my father on the pavements in early winter haze of smoke and fog. The silent echo of his footsteps endlessly reflected and then lost to the landscape.

I will drift across this city and when I'm gone my memories will trace out images of chaos on the map mirroring the mad meteors across the milkyway and rogue planets lost in the spaces between galaxies.

Lament for a Nefelibata

If history becomes fiction in being written down, then once inscribed on paper my dreams are twice removed from reality. The constellations are lost now behind the clouds. Down by the river a fish is frantically swimming upstream to avoid going over the edge. I run my hands through the sand, watching it fall through my fingers down to the surface below.

I crane my neck down and look at the sea and at the boundless ocean. They wait, unchanging. I pull in my legs and slowly get up, brushing off the sand from my clothes. The first lights of dawn are breaking over the horizon - I turn around and push myself off the beach. The air envelops me in a soft cushion and I sway in the wind like a feather lost by some bird of prey in the sky.

The sheets of ice melt from my warmth, the water gushes in around me as I plunge into the icy depths. The ice closes over me as I gently drift off into the great sea of human grief, back to the real.

CHAPTER SIX

SAILING TO KNOWHERE

Sailing a small canoe with the sails unfurled over the Aral Sea. Water as far as the eye can see, glittering Kazakh sky of sadness. The winds are cool but there is something supernatural to them. They keep growing stronger, rocking the canoe uncontrollably, until suddenly I can see the horizon. Have I reached knowhere? The horizon is shrinking. The sea is being swallowed by the sand. I try to veer the boat away from the horizon rushing towards me. The water swirling now, in its final throes, draining out in a whirlpool sinking death.

I am left in the desert with my canoe and its broken sails.

There was once an ocean here, I know, I remember. I know because I sailed it. I remember because I felt the wind on my face. I need someone to show me how to get there on foot. I can't sail the island dotted sea anymore. This desert is a stranger to me.

But I'm not fazed. It is a stranger I can come to know. The ocean too was a desert, the water and the salt, hostile and unpeopled, a desert of water. A desert brimming with secret life underneath the surface but a desert all the same. Polar deserts, Sandy deserts, Dusty deserts that you can ride across. All of them are navigable.

I can see the moon shine on the murky depths of the infinitely deep stepwell with its million cascading steps etched into the deathless rock. I can see my fears slowly taking form under the surface. And I know if I get too close to the cool green water they will pull me under. I start making my way down the steps until at last I am close enough to the water to touch it. The water is cold and evil. There is something ancient, elemental here. I pull my hand back and climb back to the surface.

The endless ruins and inns and bawdis on the way to knowhere offer not rest but the promise of an unending sleep under the cold desert moon.

In the evershift Sea of Dunes the collective footsteps of all life fade. I remember reading somewhere that the great deserts of the world are god's punishment to man. A grain of sand for every sin added to the ponds, to the lakes and now to the seas of sand. A day will come when the sand will overtake the quiet corners allotted to it and spill into our cities, flooding our Delhis and Kolkatas and Bangalores and Agras and Varanasis and after that spill over from land and into the oceans.

The scent of the old ocean in the distance. The promise of the setting sun on the horizon. The promise of great libraries on fire. The promise of time standing still on the edge of a blade. The promise of waiting for someone to watch the rain with. The promise of searching for a long lost silence. The air is struggling under their weight.

Shadows of the rain

In the valley of the moon a watchmaker sits alone on a desk of red lacquer and walnut wood. She is hunched over a small lathe nimbly working a piece of copper between her hands. Sparks burst from the metal before fading out. The air grows warm around her. It rises slowly from the smooth mosaic cracks in the flat stony plane. Dust devils glide around the valley gathering up fragments and rubble as they move around her workshop.

She can see the landscape move from the corner of her eyes. All that concerns her is the scrap of copper and the incomplete timepiece in front of her — and so she toils in the shadows of the rain alone in the valley of the moon.

By the oasis stands the temple to the sun god. And beyond that the level sand stretches out far away, resting in the cool night before a stray wind wafts them aloft and drags them into sand storms.

The broken pillars speak of great prophecy in a dead language. I imagine it speaks of dead kings and our quick movements toward the next apocalypse. Perhaps it is a dithyramb to the sun god. It might be a poem to cats or the directions to the next city. It could very well be ancient graffiti. I could spend entire nights dreaming about what the pillar might say. But I don't have countless nights. I submerge my head and drink in deeply from the oasis. Turning my head I give the place one last look and start east.

The hunters are sleeping now and the small animals have nothing to fear as they roam around the desert.

They are all huddled around the fire in the small cave. Their loose bellies flopped on the ground. It has been a long day under the Kalahari sun. The cracking flames light up the rock paintings on the walls. Outside the cave wiry plants stand guard over the sleepers.

A caravan of camels is crossing the dunes under the full moon. They move slowly against the sand. Their backs are heavy with salt, ivory and gold. The animals are alone. No traders there to recon the profits. No guards there to protect from bandits. Only the animals are there, moving solemnly through the desert leaving behind momentary footprints that are erased with the cool wind.

The lovers

My right foot bumps into something and I almost fall over. A plank of wood is poking out of the sand. I take out one of the broken oars and start moving the sand away. It is bitter work. Finally the lid of a wooden box takes shape. I jam the oar in and start prying the box open.

It is a casket. Under the wood there is a second encasing of pure continuous sapphire. The moonlight reveals a man and a woman lying inside on soft cotton. There is a look of knowing calmness on their faces. They could almost be sleeping.

I decide to let them rest under the waxing moon.

After hours of bitter work my new ship is ready. The oars fashioned into a makeshift mast are solidly mounted into the coffin lid. The sails are hanging from them, waiting. The blades of the oar are tied to the back with rope as an improvised rudder. Now all I have to do is to wait for a strong wind.

I take some sand in my hand and slowly let it drop to gauge the direction of the wind. My milkyway compass is brighter now than it has ever been. The North Star and the Three Kings are shining clearly against the Nubian sky.

The winds build up slowly, taking their time. The sails keep fluttering around undecidedly against the oars. I pick up some more sand and let it drop from my hand; it is blown away with a strong gust and the sails are taut now. I quickly align the rudder with the stars and bid farewell to the lovers.

The sea of dunes isn't kind to strangers. And it is downright malevolent to me. Taking some mercy on me the winds drop me off on the edge of a thicket. I can hear the river singing on the other side. I tie a rope to the mast and begin walking towards the sound, dragging aged wood behind me.

The sound of the river frothing and bubbling seeps into my soul. It was deep, wide and fast moving. I gingerly lower my raft into the indigo waters of the river hoping that nothing breaks the surface and tries to get me for an early breakfast. Placing my right foot on the raft, I start shifting my weight around to see if it will sink with me on it. It holds up.

Downriver from the future fine rain is sprinkling and blowing mist over the land. The wind catches me again as soon as I step down into the raft and I grab on to the mast as it bears me along. Downriver I can see narrow white waves – the rapids. One after another high foamy waves crashed through the raft.

I wake up on the shore tangled in sails, the wreckage of the raft washed up next to me. I try to untangle myself from the fabric and feel a sharp pain along the length of right arm. As I manage to get myself out I notice that splinters from the raft are poking out of my arm.

I decide to make camp on the river bank for the night, and start pulling out the splinters. Evening rolls around as I finish bandaging my hand with the fabric of the sails. I had a feeling that I wouldn't need them anymore. I dig into my bag and pull out the last of my food, biting into it with Zen pleasure and slowly moving it around my mouth.

The animals in the river are quiet now, sleeping. The forest feels taller and darker now. And as the night wears on the insects follow suit and stop chirping. The oars repurposed as kindling now are glowing as the fire crackles and the river burbles as I close my eyes.

The sun is warm on my skin and the sand has given way to solid ground. I am walking east now. After a long time it feels like my life belongs to me and to no one else. A warmth flows through me, starting at the base of my neck and making its way to my toes and fingertips.

I don't even care now where I am walking to. I walk and walk and walk and walk, passing cacti and lazy lizards resting in the warm day, paying no heed to me. The outlines of a city start taking shape. It's becoming sharper with every step.

I walk towards the city gates and almost immediately I am pulled inside the city limits by the bustling crowd around me. White flowers. That is my first impression of the town. On the walls, in flowerpots, growing out of nooks and crannies, in fenced gardens, everywhere I turn, Asphodels. I start looking around to see if I can see where I am, who these people are. There is something about their faces that unsettles me. They pass around me silent and unassuming. They don't have any words for me. And I don't have any for them. The inhabitants don't remember who they are. Do I remember who I am?

"I think you're lost", I turn around it's old whitebeard dressed in a ragged toga.

"How do you know?"

"You don't belong here", he smiles down at me.

"Where should I go then?"

"Not here. That is the way out. " He points out to the gate I have just walked through. I start walking back to the city limits, taking care to avoid the curious glances of the citizens. At the gates, people are still coming in. But I don't see any other way out of the walls. Do people never leave this place? It's harder getting out than it was getting in. I start pushing against the endless river of people flowing into the gates of the city.

As soon as I make it out, I am filled with a deep sense of loss. The walls of the city look paler now. Almost transparent. I think the city is dying. The flowers are drying up, the white vanishing from the cityscape. The buildings are decaying in front of my eyes. Slowly the tiny crannies with the flowers are blooming into fractures. The stone falling apart in fragments and the fragments weathering down to sand until there are no signs of the city left. The people linger on for a little longer with confused looks on their faces, slowly fading away into nothingness.

The mirage is broken and in the distance I can see reds and blues and solitary yellows.

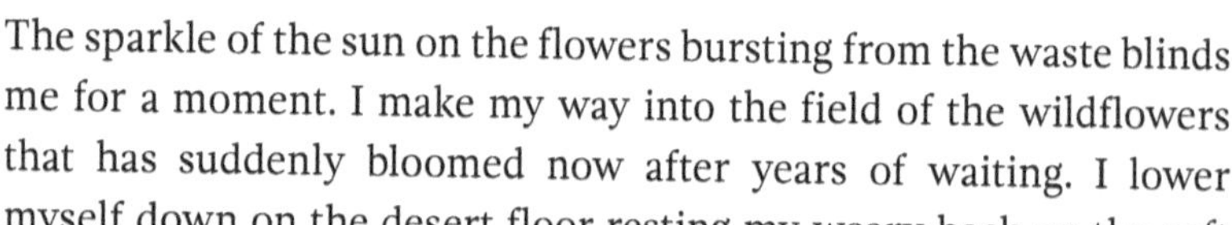

The sparkle of the sun on the flowers bursting from the waste blinds me for a moment. I make my way into the field of the wildflowers that has suddenly bloomed now after years of waiting. I lower myself down on the desert floor resting my weary back on the soft bed of flowers. I am in knowhere. It is spring now.

www.ingramcontent.com/pod-product-compliance
Lightning Source LLC
Chambersburg PA
CBHW031312130726

47988CB00007B/2809